"How did you come by them?" Feargal demanded.

"Gramps gave them to me."

"And how much do you want?"

"Want?"

"Yes, want!" he bit out. "Money, Miss Browne."

"For what? I don't understand what you're talking about."

"Such a sweet little face," he derided, his eyes cold and flat as glass. "So tailor-made for blackmail!"

Emma Richmond was born during the war in north Kent when, she says, "farms were the norm and motorways nonexistent. My childhood was one of warmth and adventure. Amiable and disorganized, I'm married with three daughters, all of whom have fled the nest—probably out of exasperation! The dog stayed, reluctantly. I'm an avid reader, a compulsive writer and a besotted new granny. I love life and my world of dreams, and all I need to make things complete is a housekeeper—like, yesterday!"

Books by Emma Richmond

HARLEQUIN PRESENTS
1516—UNFAIR ASSUMPTIONS
1582—A STRANGER'S TRUST
1669—MORE THAN A DREAM

LOVE OF
MY HEART
Emma Richmond

Harlequin Books

TORONTO • NEW YORK • LONDON
AMSTERDAM • PARIS • SYDNEY • HAMBURG
STOCKHOLM • ATHENS • TOKYO • MILAN
MADRID • WARSAW • BUDAPEST • AUCKLAND

IRELAND
Where everyone says hello,
and getting lost is an eternal delight.

ISBN 0-373-03349-4

LOVE OF MY HEART

Copyright © 1993 by Emma Richmond.

First North American Publication 1995.

Printed in U.S.A.

CHAPTER ONE

'IT'S HARRY!'

'Harry?' Ellie queried in bewilderment, but the woman wasn't listening, just staring—well, almost malevolently after a man in a tan jacket.

'And if he's thinking he'll be getting away with it he can think again! Mind the stall for a minute, will you, love?' Without waiting for an answer, she dashed off along the street and after the rapidly departing Harry.

'Hey,' Ellie called after her weakly, 'I don't know anything about serving on stalls...' and then let her hand drop limply to her side. Why her? she wondered. The woman didn't even know she could trust her, for goodness' sake! She could run off with all the stock! And what evil demon had prompted her to drive past a street market which all the gods knew she couldn't resist? Really, Ellie, you are the limit, she scolded herself. All you had to do was drive off the ferry, find the main road, and drive straight to Dublin. Simple. So what did you do? Stopped, just for five minutes, just to have a quick look, and now here you are, in charge of the stall of a woman you don't know, a woman you've never seen before in your life, and all because someone called Harry wasn't to get away with something— And that man with blue eyes was watching her again. Oh, heavens. Turning away from a regard that seemed faintly menacing, she tried to look as though she knew what she was doing as she rearranged some sweaters.

Two people lingered, fingering the scarves, and she put her head down, feigning ignorance, or ineptitude, or just plain stupidity—whatever, so long as they went away without asking her the price of anything! It obviously worked, because they mumbled something and moved on. Aware of still being watched, she glanced up cautiously. Ole blue eyes again. Oh, please don't let him be a thief, she prayed; please don't let him run off with all the woman's stock. Peeping sideways at him, she decided he definitely looked menacing. Tall, loose-limbed, black hair, the stuff of heroes—or villains. Blue, blue eyes that captured and held your glance. A look to make your knees go weak, and—oh, hell—he was coming this way. He looked arrogant, brooding—dangerous? And he halted in front of her.

'It leaks,' he said without preamble, and in one of those soft seductive voices that sort of oozed through your pores.

'I beg your pardon?' she queried weakly.

'It leaks,' he repeated.

'What does?'

'My coat.'

'Oh.' Dear heaven, he wasn't the local lunatic, was he? Cautiously glancing around her, seeing how many people were in earshot should she need to shout, she turned back with a lame smile. 'I'm sorry.'

'Yes.'

'What?' she asked in confusion.

'You told me it was guaranteed waterproof.'

'I didn't! I've never seen you before in my life!'

'No,' he agreed softly.

'Then why in h—?'

'Figuratively speaking, I meant. I bought it a few months ago and I was assured they were waterproof.'

'And they aren't?'

'No.'

'Perhaps you were just unlucky and got a rogue one,' she offered helplessly.

'Perhaps.'

'I can't give you a refund,' she blurted. 'It's not my stall!'

'I know.'

'Then what *do* you want?' she demanded in exasperation.

'From you? At the moment? Nothing.'

Staring at him in bewildered astonishment, she searched his face. Was he one of those people who told jokes with a perfectly straight face so that you didn't know if it was a joke or not? He didn't *look* as though he was joking.

'And if you don't mind my saying so,' he continued in that same soft, gentle voice, so at variance with his appearance, 'you appear to give to sales what vampires might give to the transfusion service.'

Chagrin struggling with honesty, she gave a doubtful little smile that was enormously appealing. 'Mm,' she agreed. 'Kiss-of-Death Lil, that's me. But I don't know anything *about* selling things, only before I could tell that to the woman who owns the stall she'd rushed off to follow someone called Harry—who's not getting away with it,' she tacked on comically. 'So I'm sorry if I can't help you. Perhaps you could come back later.'

'No need,' he denied. With a look that she didn't know what to make of at all, he walked across to the revolving stand that held coats much like the one he was wearing, removed the sign that said 'Guaranteed Waterproof', and tore it in half. And suddenly the devil was in his eyes and in his smile. Such a wicked, wicked smile. Handing her the pieces, he sketched a little salute, and strolled away.

A delightful, if somewhat bewildered smile tugging at her own mouth, her eyes alight with laughter, she watched him melt into the crowds. Oh, boy.

'All right, dear?'

Swinging round, she stared rather blankly at the stall-holder. Glancing down at the torn card, she gave a little moue of apology. 'He tore your sign in half!' she exclaimed weakly.

'Who did?'

'That man.' Turning, she searched the crowds for a glimpse of him. Unable to see him, she sighed. 'Well, a man, anyway. He said they weren't waterproof.'

'No more they are,' she grinned.

'Oh.' With a little giggle, Ellie asked curiously, 'Did you catch up with Harry?'

'I did!' she exclaimed in obvious satisfaction. 'And if he thought he could get away with cheating our Sheila he was very much mistaken! However, the man's a fool and she'll be better off without him.'

An hour later she was still happily chatting to the woman, finding out about the terrible Harry who had 'torn the heart' right out of her daughter and gone off with a woman from Cork, which naturally led on to the dreadful and often incomprehensible ways of men and the stupid way women always put up with it. By the time Ellie did finally remember she was supposed to be meeting someone in Dublin, the afternoon was well advanced.

'I must go,' she said regretfully, 'I shall be awfully late.'

'Sure, and isn't everyone?' she laughed. 'Go on, away with you; thank you for your help, you've been grand.'

With a happy smile on her extraordinarily beautiful face, and the memory of a man with blue eyes in her mind, she wandered back to where she had left her car, and Ellie being Ellie, who was totally incapable of passing anything that looked even remotely interesting, it was another hour before she finally got to it. The drive up to Dublin was, naturally, not without its problems.

Pulling up outside the hotel, she gave a big, thankful sigh. Only three hours late, she thought ruefully. Lord, but Ireland was a confusing place. Staring out at the low grey sky, the drizzle that hadn't stopped once on the journey up from Wexford, she jammed on her hat. Where was the summer?

Collecting her bits and pieces, she climbed from the car, locked it, and, as she turned, collided with someone. Bright blue eyes regarded her without expression. Blue eyes that made it hard to look away. Blue eyes that made her heart give an alarming little lurch. Gone was the waxed jacket and jeans, replaced by a dinner-jacket that made him look formal and distinguished—and even more dangerously attractive.

With a wide, delighted smile, because she hadn't really expected ever to see him again, she teased, 'Are you following me?'

The look he gave her made her feel extremely stupid—and disappointed. 'Why would I be following you?' he asked quietly.

'I don't know,' she mumbled. 'Sorry.'

His steady regard continued for what seemed like an eternity, and she *thought* there was a little flash of amusement in his eyes, but then he gave a tiny dip of his

head, and she was no longer sure. With him still carefully shielding his female companion with a large umbrella, they moved off toward the hotel entrance. Tall,
black-haired, devastating. The sort of looks that fuelled
dreams. The sort of looks that broke hearts. Ah, well.
Tugging her hat straight, Ellie followed them into the
hotel. Rather a coincidence, though, wasn't it? And
he'd looked at her as though he'd never seen her before
in his life. Perhaps he didn't remember he had. Once
seen and forever forgotten, she thought wryly. Well,
that would scotch any conceit she might be tempted to
have!

He kindly held the door for her. Well, perhaps not
kindly, she decided; it was more along the lines of au-
tomatic courtesy, done without thought, and the moment he saw she had the door he moved away, his hand
once more at his companion's elbow. They were both in
evening dress, as were most of the people in the very
crowded foyer. Trust her to arrive slap-bang in the
middle of someone's function. Glancing down at her
own rather crumpled appearance, she hid a smile. And
where was Donal Sullivan in all this? she wondered.
Would he have given her up as lost? And if he hadn't,
would she even recognise him? She'd only met him
once, and then only briefly. He was her friend Maura's
brother, who lived in Dublin, and who, Maura assured
her, would be delighted to show her the town. Ho, hum.
Did all sisters lend their brothers out as though they
were books? She had no idea. She didn't have a brother.
Dragging her mind back to the matter in hand, and
mumbling apologies, she wormed her way to the reception desk.

She was greeted with a sympathetic, and rather amused smile. But then most people viewed Ellie with a smile. She was that sort of person.

'Hi,' she greeted breathlessly as she tugged off her deplorable hat. 'Sorry I'm so late. I got lost. And if I never, ever see St Stephen's Green again it will be far too soon!' she exclaimed with an endearing little grin. 'Why did no one ever tell me Dublin was all one-way streets? And I'm parked on a yellow line, and it's raining—and I'm Elinor Browne, with an "E",' she concluded in a little rush.

'Hello, Elinor Browne with an "E",' the receptionist said softly, her brown eyes full of laughter. 'And being late is no problem at all.' When a crowd of people surged from a side-room, all talking and laughing, she pulled a face of mock-exasperation. 'Sure and wouldn't you arrive in the middle of this débâcle? A convention in one room, a wedding reception in another, and neither wanting to stay where they were put.'

Glancing round at the noisy throng, Ellie observed helpfully, 'I expect they find each other's groups more interesting.'

'And isn't that the truth? Oh, well, I'm not about to try and separate them. You have luggage?'

'Yes, outside. Is there a car park I should move the car to?'

'John will do it; you'll not be wanting to go back out in the rain.' Beckoning over a young man, whose look of boredom miraculously changed to one of interest when he saw Ellie, the receptionist gave a wry smile before instructing, 'If you'll give him your car keys, he'll park it for you and take your luggage up to your room—and don't give him *more* than your car keys,' she added with friendly warning. 'Give an inch and that

one will take a mile.' Sliding a registration card towards her, she offered a pen. 'Dining-room to your
right, bar to the left, lift behind the columns,' she continued helpfully. 'Dinner finished early this evening
because of the convention, but there'll be snacks in the
bar if you're hungry. Now, what else? Breakfast from
seven till ten—and anything else you'll be needing, no
doubt you'll be asking,' she concluded warmly.

'Yes, thank you.' Enormously impressed by this
friendly, helpful girl, who didn't seem in the least like
most receptionists she encountered, Ellie slid back the
registration card, accepted her plastic key, gave one of
her funny little smiles, and decided that before going up
to her room she'd better try and find Donal.

Turning too fast, she knocked someone's black-clad
arm, and the drink he was holding spilled. Looking up
quickly, her apology already forming, she slowly closed
her mouth. In the artificial light of the hotel, his blue
eyes looked brighter, more penetrating. Offering him a
hesitant smile, which wasn't returned, she gave a little
grimace and tried to edge away, not easy in that crush.

'Is it a vendetta?' he asked softly.

'What?' Staring back up into his face, and seeing
nothing, no humour, no teasing, she was a little non-
plussed. 'No,' she denied lamely.

'And did you have no electricity?' he probed in the
same soft, lilting voice.

'Electricity?' she echoed, still mesmerised by his
bright blue eyes.

'Mm.'

'Well, yes,' she mumbled confusedly, 'Didn't you?'

'Certainly I did, but then I don't look as though I
dressed all by guess. Do I?'

'Oh. No.' Relieved to find that he must be joking after all, she gave her enchanting little grin. 'Courtesy of charity shops,' she confessed.

'Which still doesn't explain why nothing matches.'

'It doesn't?'

'No.'

'Pink doesn't go with purple?'

'Ye-s, but not that particular shade, and not when it's teamed with yellow.'

'Know about women's fashions, do you?' she teased.

'No, but I know about colour.'

'And these colours don't suit me?'

His head on one side, he gave a slight inclination of his head. 'Yes, for some odd, inexplicable reason they do, and that's what I find so extraordinary, because I can't imagine you dressed in any other way. I don't know why I can't, but fashionable clothes, would, I think, make you fade, make you ordinary, and you quite clearly aren't.' Glancing down, his gaze encompassed her very odd person. 'Men's working boots, black ribbed tights, a purple cotton skirt, pink overlarge cardigan, and a yellow scarf are, for some extraordinary reason, you.'

'I also have a green velvet hat,' she told him solemnly, holding it up for inspection.

'Yes. It looks like one Henry the Eighth might have discarded for reasons of vanity. Tell me your name,' he commanded.

'Elinor.'

'Doesn't suit you.'

'No, but then how do you ever know that your dear little baby isn't going to grow up to be tall and elegant?' she quipped with huge enjoyment. It had been a long time since she'd met anyone even remotely interesting, and whatever this man was he certainly wasn't remote!

'Are your parents tall and elegant?'

'Yes.' With another of her tiny smiles that somehow looked both secretive and inviting, she told him, 'Most people call me Ellie.'

'Then I shall count myself among them. My name is Feargal.'

'Fergie?' she asked in delight.

'No,' he reproved sternly, 'Feargal.' Moving his gaze past her, he sighed. 'And now I must go; I see my companion is waiting—and not very patiently. Please excuse me.' He turned away, and then turned back. There was a fascinating little indentation beside his mouth. Prelude to a smile? 'But I'll find you again, Ellie,' he said softly. It sounded like a promise.

Her eyes riveted on his broad back, she gave a slow, naughty smile as she watched him thread his way towards his elegant companion. Would he? Find her again? She found herself hoping very much that he would. He was—interesting, and looked as though he knew his way around the world both backwards and forwards, including the inside of a lady's bedroom—not that she was intending to let him inside *her* bedroom, but it might be fun to indulge in a little flirtation, mightn't it? She was on holiday after all, and it certainly seemed as though that was what he'd been indulging in while waiting for his ladyfriend to return. Funny that they'd both been heading for the same place, though. Aware that the receptionist was watching her, she gave an embarrassed little smile. 'Pretty devastating, huh?'

'Indeed he is. Wicked.'

Yes, she agreed silently. Wicked. Wickedly attractive. Wickedly intriguing. Go and find Donal, Ellie, she
told herself sternly, instead of mooning over a man you
know nothing about and probably wouldn't like if you
did. Right. Although she bet she would like him. With
another little smile, she moved away in search of her
future, if temporary guide.

The wedding party still seemed happily merged with
the convention, and, without having any choice in the
matter, Ellie was absorbed into the friendly crowd. A
drink was thrust into her hand and within five minutes
she was being passed from group to group as though she
were the prize exhibit; asked numerous questions she
didn't know how to or have time to answer; told endless tales of this person or that person; until eventually,
somewhat bewildered, she ended up in the bar with
someone called Patrick who began regaling her with
tales of old Ireland. She *thought* he was probably pulling her leg, but wouldn't actually have laid money on
it—and it was there, seated at the bar, that Donal finally found her.

'Ellie?'

Swinging round, she grinned in relief. 'Donal? Well,
thank goodness for that. I was beginning to wonder if
I'd ever find you!'

'Me, too,' he confessed with a warm, relieved smile.
'But where on earth have you been? I've been searching all over for you! I was beginning to wonder if
something had happened, and then wondered how the
devil I was going to tell Maura if it had! Was the ferry
late?'

'No,' she denied with a wry little smile, 'the ferry was
perfectly on time; it was your wretched Dublin streets

that were the problem! Someone might have warned me they were all one-way!'

'It's never taken you six hours to get from Rosslare to here!' he exclaimed in disbelief.

'Well, no,' she admitted sheepishly, 'I got a bit way-laid in Wexford. They had a market,' she added, as though that would immediately explain all.

Laughing delightedly, he shook his head at her. 'And didn't Maura warn me that life generally got very complicated when you were around?' Eyeing her newfound companions sitting at her other side, and who were avid listeners to their conversation, he resumed wryly, 'And that within five minutes of you arriving anywhere you had the entire population at your feet, knew their life histories, their problems...'

'Oh, what a fib.'

With an attractive chuckle, he took the seat beside her, and, attracting the barman's attention, ordered their drinks.

A smile still hovering round her mouth, she glanced up and through the mirror. Blue, blue eyes caught and held hers, and she burst into delighted laughter.

Without taking his eyes from hers, Feargal tapped Donal lightly on the shoulder. 'Mine's whisky.'

Swinging round in astonishment, Donal exclaimed, 'What on earth are you doing here? I thought you were supposed to be at the gallery! Although I might have known you'd arrive just as drinks were being ordered! You have the devil's own timing, Feargal.'

'Mm,' he agreed without answering anything he'd been asked.

'And this,' Donal added in obvious amusement when Feargal's eyes didn't once waver from his companion, 'is Ellie!'

'Yes,' he agreed softly. 'This is Ellie.'

'You've met?'

'Mm.'

Staring at Feargal, and then at Ellie, Donal's smile widened infectiously. 'You never went to find her at Rosslare? That was meant to be a joke!'

'I know,' he admitted, his eyes still on Ellie. 'But I was bored.'

'Bored?' she echoed. Looking from one to the other, she asked slowly, 'You followed me from the ferry?'

'Mm.'

'Knew who I was?'

'Mm.'

'But you just asked—in Reception—what my name was!'

'Mm.'

'Why?'

'I told you,' he drawled laconically, 'I was bored—and you amused me.'

Not entirely sure she wanted to be the object of someone's amusement, or a reliever of boredom, she gave him back stare for stare. And the wretch smiled.

'Get bored with your fair companion too, did you?' she asked sweetly.

'Oh, I've always been bored with Delores.'

Well, there wasn't a lot of answer to that, was there? And as a conversation-stopper, that little remark won hands down.

'Then why, my friend,' Donal asked softly, 'did you drag her round here?'

Switching his gaze to the younger man, Feargal gave a slow smile. There was a wealth of meaning in that smile, one not entirely lost on Ellie.

Shaking his head at Feargal, amusement dancing in his eyes, Donal turned back to the barman and Ellie was left with only her drink, or Feargal, to stare at. She chose the latter.

'They should have called you Helen,' he observed quietly.

'They should? Why?'

'Because you have a face that might have launched a thousand ships. Eyes of darkest brown,' he continued softly, but he didn't sound as though he were amused, or teasing—rather as though he was merely making a statement of fact, which she found slightly disconcerting. 'A face the fairies would be proud to call their own. No, not fairies—elves; you have an elfin look.'

'Pointy ears?' she queried lightly.

'No, but if you had they would suit you. Have you ever had your hair long?' he asked idly.

She'd lost count of the number of people who'd asked her that; lost count of the number of answers she'd given. Running her hand over what was left of thick, dark hair that had been shaved to within half an inch of its life and which served to enhance her astonishingly beautiful face, she smiled. 'It needs cutting.'

Lazily lifting his hand, he trailed his fingers over her scalp, and a tingle went down to her toes. 'Like fur,' he commented before his attention shifted abruptly towards the doorway. With a look of resignation, he removed his hand, took his glass from Donal, and, that fascinating little indent beside his mouth once more in evidence, he moved off towards the beckoning Dolores.

With another chuckle, Donal clicked his glass against hers. '*Sláinte.*'

'*Sláinte,*' she echoed, and hoped it meant what she thought it meant.

'What time did you want to leave tomorrow? Maura said you were driving up north.'

'Mm. Slane.'

'Yes, Slane,' he agreed on a little choke of laughter.

'Going to Slane is funny?' she asked in some bewilderment.

'No, no,' he denied. 'Got somewhere to stay?'

'I've got a list of bed and breakfasts. The tourist office said I wouldn't have any trouble finding somewhere.'

'No, you should be all right,' he agreed, his smile still in place, 'but you'd best leave after lunch tomorrow to give yourself plenty of time—just in case you get sidetracked,' he added, tongue-in-cheek.

'Ha, ha.' Returning her gaze to dark hair and broad shoulders, she asked, 'What did you mean about it being a joke? About Feargal coming to find me at Rosslare? I assumed it was coincidence, seeing him in Wexford, and then finding him staying in the same hotel. But it obviously wasn't.'

'No, and he isn't staying in the same hotel.'

'He isn't?'

'No.'

'So?' she persisted in exasperation.

With a broad smile, he explained, 'When I was talking to him the other day, and I happened to mention that an old friend of my sister's was coming to Ireland, and that I was going to show her round Dublin, and that we'd agreed to meet here, and about how scatty...'

'I am not scatty,' she denied.

'Yes, you are—and about how astonishingly beautiful you were... Yes, you are! You know you are, so don't bother to deny it, and I said you were arriving on the Rosslare ferry and...'

'And added that you hoped I had enough intelli-
gence to actually find Dublin!' she finished for him.
'Thank you so much!'

Unrepentant, he nodded. 'And Feargal said he would
be down there that day, and I said—you know how you
do—if you happen to see a dark green Morris Minor
driven by this astonishingly beautiful girl with cropped
dark hair, would you make sure she gets on the right
road? And he obviously did, and—well, there you are.'

Staring at him, and then back to the retreating form
of Feargal, she agreed drily, 'Yes, there we are.' Yet
what really were the chances of seeing the very car you'd
been asked to look out for? True, there were very few
Morris Minors around, and if you saw one you'd probably remember it; but to follow it into Wexford? Seek
her out in the market? She wasn't *that* beautiful. And
he'd been bored ... A wry, self-mocking smile playing
about her mouth, her eyes still riveted on thick dark
hair, she asked absently, 'So who is he, this man who
follows unknown women? And what is he doing here?'

'Having a drink?'

'Donal!'

With a laugh, he relented. 'I imagine he came in here
to see his little friend Ellie again. I can't think of any
other reason for him to walk out of the dinner he was
supposed to be at. And as for who he is ... oh, farmer,
racehorse owner, playboy, landowner, owns a big
house—the gardens of which, to everyone's amusement,' he added with his infectious chuckle, 'he opens
to the public.'

'Why to everyone's amusement?'

'Because although it's a handsome house, and the
gardens are extensive, they in no way compare to those
of the castle which is just up the road.'

'Which is also open to the public?'

'Yes. Feargal reckoned that if tourists would pay to see the castle they might very well pay to see his garden.'

'And do they?'

'Oh, yes,' he laughed. 'He has the charm and the luck of Old Nick himself. And, still not to be outdone, he then opened a restaurant, in direct competition with the castle.'

'And that pays enough to keep him?' she asked curiously. He'd looked as though he had expensive tastes. She didn't know how she knew that; she just did. He also looked sophisticated and worldly—and far out of the reach of someone like Ellie Browne. He was obviously well-known here in Dublin. She'd seen people nod to him, shake his hand. One of the smart set? The wealthy set?

'No,' Donal denied, 'they don't get that many tourists up—er—where he lives. People mostly go to the west coast. I imagine most of his income comes from farming. Although his horses do seem to win quite often. Intrigued, Ellie?' he teased.

Not bothering to admit or deny it, she merely smiled. 'A case of you name it and Feargal probably dabbles in it?'

'Something like that.'

'He's famous?'

'Well, well-known, at any rate.'

'And Dolores?'

'Oh, Dolores is an artist. Feargal's her sponsor, or patron, or whatever you call it, and whenever there's an exhibition, or a dinner, like the one tonight, when up-and-coming artists are wined and dined, he has to attend—or is supposed to,' he added drily. 'To give her credit, she is an excellent artist, probably one of our top painters.'

'Oh.' Not his ladyfriend, then. But if he was wealthy, and well-known, he was hardly likely to look twice at herself, was he? So why had he? she wondered, with an intriguing little smile. Because he really was bored? Jaded? And a little English girl might provide light relief? Not that she was ever likely to see him again after today. Pity, that; he might have been—fun.

'And just why are you wearing that secret little smile, my friend?' Donal queried softly.

'No reason,' she lied. 'So, what are the arrangements for tomorrow?'

Allowing her to change the subject, he offered, 'Shall I meet you in the foyer after breakfast, say nine-thirty? Then we can spend the morning looking at the shops, have lunch in a nice restaurant, and then I'll point you in the right direction for Slane. Is that all right?'

'Very much so. Thank you. You truly don't mind showing me around? Maura didn't blackmail you into it?'

'No blackmail needed, Ellie. It will be my pleasure.'

'Then thank you.'

'Welcome. Maura said you were going up to Slane to look up some old friends of the family; is that right?'

'Yes,' she agreed without elaborating, because although it was true it wasn't entirely the truth, and she hoped he would have the good manners not to probe further. He did, and with a relieved smile she turned back to talk to her new-found friends on her other side, and within half an hour, to Donal's exasperated amusement, had quite a crowd round her, all vying with each other to tell her stories.

By the time she eventually got up to her room, she was out on her feet, and, if she were honest, not entirely sober. Undressing, she tumbled naked into the wide bed, and within seconds was fast asleep.

When she woke in the morning, it was to clear blue skies, and she gave a sigh of pleasure. She also remembered the man with blue eyes. Feargal—who'd been bored. And if he was a prime example of the country's men ... Sure, and wasn't Ireland a delightful place altogether? Chuckling, she glanced at her watch, then quickly climbed from the bed and padded into the luxurious bathroom. Sampling all the expensive-looking sachets, courtesy of the hotel, she had a nice refreshing shower, and, still wrapped in a bath sheet, repacked her case. Making sure that the precious package that she had come all this way to deliver was still safely at the bottom, she dressed in comfortable jeans, and what looked like a man's old-fashioned sleeved vest, dyed red, and she was ready. Leaving her case to be collected, she took the lift down to the ground floor, and, in her usual fashion, hovered indecisively just inside the dining-room door. She looked little, and helpless, and totally out of place—and none of it was true. It wasn't that she had ever made a conscious decision to play the helpless female; she just always looked as though she was in constant need of care and attention, and over the years she had found that it was far easier to allow people to think what they liked, because whenever she tried to be assertive, or explain that she was really quite competent, no one ever believed her.

With a wide smile, one of the waitresses came to collect her, and seat her at a small table in the window.

'Now, what would you like? Something light?'

With a wry little smile, Ellie shook her head. 'I'll have the full breakfast, please.'

Looking extremely dubious, the waitress explained, 'That's cereal, egg and bacon, toast and coffee.'

'Yes, that would be lovely, but not the bacon. Could I have tomatoes instead?'

'Oh, yes, of course.' Still looking doubtful, she went off to fill the order, and when Ellie had eaten it all, down to the very last scrap, and had two cups of coffee, she came back to stand at the table, full of admiration and amazement. 'And won't that teach me to make judgements?' she asked with a laugh. 'You don't look as though you could even manage half a slice of toast.'

Amusement lurking in her dark eyes, because that's what people always said, Ellie signed the bill, thanked the waitress, gave her a warm smile, added a little tip, and went out to wait for Donal.

Dublin was a happy town, Ellie decided, although Grafton Street, the main shopping area, she found a little disappointing because the shops weren't so very different from those at home. However, she did go into the famous Bewley's Coffee House, for the equally famous potato soup. She viewed the Regency houses in Merrion Square, Donal an amused and willing companion; solemnly inspected Trinity College, and looked at the Liffey River. She also saw the statue of Molly Malone, minus wheelbarrow, which made her laugh. And a morning was not nearly long enough to explore the friendly and fascinating city. She would come back, she promised herself, on her way home.

Thanking Donal for his kindness, and giving him a friendly hug, she dutifully took the road he indicated—and then Ellie, being Ellie, decided wouldn't it be nice just to have a peek at the Wicklow mountains? She could make just a small detour... She had a decent map, didn't she? Turning her little Morris Minor back through the busy and confusing streets, she recrossed the river, and took a side-road towards the distant mountain range. Which was why she didn't arrive on the outskirts of Slane until it was nearly dark.

She eventually found the River Boyne, which, according to the map, ran near Slane—which was probably a lie, she decided after making numerous unlooked-for detours because the map didn't seem to bear any relation to the roads, which didn't seem to be signposted—except for one that explained where the famous battle had taken place. On yet another impulse, she stopped to have a quick look, because it just might have mentioned where Slane was, mightn't it? It didn't, and by the time she did reach the village it was fully dark—and pouring with rain. Promising herself that she would explore it all properly later, she set off to find accommodation. Which she foolishly assumed would be easy, because she had foolishly assumed that Irish villages were like English ones. They weren't. Or at least this one wasn't. It was far smaller for one thing—and unbelievably empty. The name of the local pub, Live and Let Live, seemed like a good omen the first time she drove past it. But not by the third time. Where was everybody? Why was there no one to ask? Driving over the wide crossroads, for the second time, without another car to be seen, she had a vision of herself driving around all night.

Past the looming castle again, somehow sinister in the driving rain—and there, finally, thankfully, tucked away in the hedge, was a little sign. 'Bed and Breakfast'. Sending up eternal thanks to whatever deity happened to be in residence, she turned into the lane, which probably in sunlight, or at least daylight, was pretty, but which in the car's headlights looked waterlogged, thankfully parked, stretched her cramped muscles, dragged on her hat, and got out. Sadly, her thoughts of a good omen continued to prove false, because no sooner had she raised the knocker than the door was wrenched open, and a young woman emerged backwards, still talking to someone inside the house. Or arguing.

'Sure and doesn't everything go wrong when you least expect it? I don't know whether I'm coming or going! And don't forget to turn the light out!'

Plunged suddenly into darkness, Ellie blinked to accustom her eyes, opened her mouth—and closed it again.

'And why the devil we have to rush off at a moment's notice, I don't know...'

'Yes, you do, Michael Ryan. Didn't I just say it was Sadie?'

'No...'

'And didn't she ring to demand we go there not half an hour since?'

'I don't know,' he denied in exasperation. 'Did she?'

'And wasn't she that desperate that I didn't have the heart to tell her no?' Turning to face front, she suddenly saw Ellie and gave a little screech of alarm. 'Lord, but you frightened me half to death!'

'Sorry,' Ellie mumbled lamely. 'Do you...?'

'Lost, are you?' she asked kindly.

'Well, no...'

'And there's me rambling on and you not knowing who the devil I am, nor me you...'

'And not likely to find out,' the young man who emerged dragging a suitcase muttered, 'if you don't give the poor girl a chance to finish a thing she's saying.'

'Sorry,' she laughed. 'How can I help?'

'I was looking for somewhere to stay, but if you're—'

'Stay? Well, would you believe it!' she exclaimed in disgust. 'Months we've been open, and not one enquiry, and the minute we do get one we can't take her in! Now what to do?' Seemingly oblivious to the rain, she stood in thought for a moment. 'Meg's no good—she's away—and you won't want to be driving far at this time of night...'

When the front door slammed behind them, and the young man joined them on the step, she asked, 'What about the Hall? They...'

'The Hall?' he exclaimed. 'But—'

'And don't they have rooms enough to house an army?' she demanded just as though he was about to deny it. 'And don't they sometimes take in paying guests?'

'Well, yes...'

'Yes,' she agreed firmly. Turning back to Ellie, she asked, 'Did you want to stay long?'

'A few days, a week...'

'Then that will be best,' she said authoritatively. 'Come on.' Leaving the man to lug the case, she led the way down the path. 'If you go back down the lane, turn right, then quick right again, you'll see the Hall. You knock there; they'll set you right. Say Annie sent you. I'm really sorry we couldn't help, but if you're still here in a couple of days, and still need somewhere, we should be back by then. I hope,' she muttered under her breath.

'Oh, right, yes, thank you.' With a quick smile, and not really having any choice, Ellie climbed back into her car, turned on the muddy track, and went back the way she'd come.

The Hall didn't sound the sort of place—well, the sort of place that might be cheap. And although Grams had left her enough money for just this purpose she'd been hoping to live cheaply so that she could stay in Ireland for at least a month, see as much of the country as she could. On the other hand, driving round at night, in the pouring rain, didn't appeal either. Perhaps she could stay just the one night, then look for something cheaper in the morning.

CHAPTER TWO

ELLIE FOUND THE HALL easily enough, parked tidily on the gravel, and then just sat and stared at it. Impressive was the first word that sprang to mind. Ducal. A large grey stone mansion, surrounded by rhododendrons. Not at all the sort of place for little Ellie Browne. There was no board outside proclaiming it to be a guest house, or hotel, so if it wasn't, and they only took in private guests, or friends, she could hardly go dumping herself on them on the recommendation of someone called Annie, could she? On the other hand, neither could she spend the night in the car in their front garden. Oh, well, nothing ventured, nothing gained. Straightening her hat, she picked up her bag, and climbed out.

Marching across the gravel, she knocked firmly on the vast front door. A dog barked, and someone shouted. And after what seemed like an eternity the door opened—and she stared in surprise and disbelief at the tall black-haired man with the blue, blue eyes.

'Well, well, well, if it isn't Ellie Browne,' he drawled softly. 'Now why aren't I surprised?'

'I don't know,' she denied in confusion. 'You should be—I am!' And, correctly interpreting his expression, she added forcefully, 'And if that look you're giving me means what I think it means—it doesn't! Because I'm not!'

'Not?' he asked softly.

'No. I've never followed anyone in my life, and certainly have no intention of starting now. I didn't know—I mean…' But Donal had—that was more than obvious; that's why he'd laughed. The little wretch. It was also presumably why he'd sent Feargal off to Wexford, as a joke, because he'd known damn well that he lived in Slane and that Ellie was likely to meet him again. Not that she'd be actually knocking on his door, of course—if indeed it was his door—but certainly that she was likely to meet him.

Still staring up at him, she tried to discover if he was making the same connections as herself, but his face gave absolutely nothing away, and yet, when he'd first opened the door, she'd thought he'd looked disappointed. Because he'd been expecting someone else? Although why he should think that, she couldn't imagine—unless women were in the habit of following him home. He was dressed in a blue shirt and jeans, which should have made him look more relaxed, and didn't. He looked sort of sternly amused, if there was such an expression, and really rather imposing, and as he continued to regard her she saw there was a glitter in his eyes, which could have been amusement, she supposed, if one were very optimistic. It could also have been irritation. 'You're not staying here, are you?' she asked fatalistically. 'This is your house. Right?'

'Right,' he agreed blandly.

'And all because of the wretched Sadie!' she retorted in disgust.

'Sadie?' he queried.

'Mm. She was desperate.'

His beautifully shaped mouth gave an infinitesimal twitch, and she relaxed slightly before rushing into an explanation. 'Annie up the road told me to come here;

she said that you sometimes take in paying guests—and there wasn't anywhere else, and it was dark, and raining—but it obviously isn't a very good idea, so if you could tell me where else to try—I'll go and try,' she concluded lamely.

'Now why would you be wanting to do that?' he asked in lazy amusement.

'Because you think I followed you up here, and I didn't, because it's not fair, because you're not a hotel, are you? And because I can't just dump myself on complete strangers...'

'But we're not complete strangers, are we? And as for being fair, well, no one else ever seems to find it a problem.'

'They don't?' she asked in confusion.

'No. Come on, you'd best come inside. Where's your case?'

'In the car.' Hanging back as he strode off to get it, she protested worriedly, 'I really think it might be best not to—and I don't know quite how it is, but although you all seem to move without speed, not to hurry, I feel as though I'm being rushed along without time to draw breath!'

'I know the feeling,' he agreed with that fascinating little indent beside his mouth as he returned with her case. 'Come on.'

'Are you sure? I don't want to be a nuisance...'

'You don't?'

'No,' she denied confusedly as she reluctantly followed him through the side-door. What did that mean? That he wanted her to be a nuisance? She wished people wouldn't talk in riddles. It was very confusing. And to have met him on her own terms, or by accident, would have been one thing, and a delight, but to look as though she were some silly teenager following an idol ... well, that was entirely another. And what were the chances of persuading him that it really was coincidence? She didn't know; it was hard to tell with this man; she could never see what he was thinking. She didn't know why that bothered her, but it did.

Chewing on her lower lip, she trundled after him along a flagged passageway and up an ornate wooden staircase. Walking along the top landing, he flung open a door at the end, and stood back for her to enter.

It looked the sort of room Queen Anne might have spent a night in. The sort of room you might show visitors round, and at the thought of a stream of visitors politely filing in while she was still in bed she gave a little grin.

'You don't like it?' he asked softly.

'Oh, yes, it's lovely. Just—um—'

'Overpowering? Ornate? Old?' he queried helpfully in his soft, rather musical voice that sent funny little shivers up and down her spine.

'Yes,' she agreed lamely as she stared somewhat helplessly at the enormous four-poster bed that dominated the room. The furniture looked antique, the carpet priceless and Ellie hastily examined the soles of her boots before daring to step on it—and Feargal's eyes suddenly warmed with laughter.

'Poor Ellie,' he commiserated softly, then, with an all-encompassing gesture, invited casually, 'Do what you like, wander where you will. We have no other guests at the moment, only family, so you must take us as you find us, eat with us, drink with us—make love with us.' The laughter still in his eyes, he put her case on the ottoman at the foot of the bed, turned and went out.

Make love? Oh, heavens, just the thought of it made her feel positively puttyfied. And why on earth had he said it? Because he did find her attractive? Or because he was still bored? And because he thought she had followed him for just that purpose? But it had been coincidence. All of it. Not contrived on her part at all. But, judging by his attitude, he clearly wasn't going to believe that. Small blame to him, of course; it would be difficult for anyone to believe it. And if Donal had been there right at that moment she might have thumped him. And why had he said, 'Poor Ellie,' in that odiously knowing way? What on earth did he think he knew that she didn't?

With a tired shake of her head, she practically tiptoed across to the window and looked out. She couldn't see any other lights twinkling in the distance that might indicate other dwellings, so perhaps the grounds were extensive. Very extensive. Woodland? Parkland? Perhaps he ran a herd of beef—cows or something. Donal said he farmed. Was this the farm? Peering through the dark window, her hand cupped to the pane, she made out what looked like two rather sad and bedraggled horses standing beneath an enormous oak, heads hung low. Perhaps they'd met Sadie. Who was desperate. And if they were horses, why weren't they in a barn or something? Didn't you have to put horses away at night—like a car?

With a snort of laughter, she returned to her case and humped it on to the bed. Welcome to Ireland, and their comfortable, confusing, delightful brand of hospitality— And did they always keep this room made up for guests? Feargal hadn't asked anyone where she was to be put, just brought her up here. Perhaps it was his room... Oh, don't be so stupid, Ellie!

He'd also mentioned family. How many family? Brothers? Sisters? Mother? Wife? Children? Yes, and why hadn't that occurred to her before—that he might be married with children? Because he'd flirted with her? Because she was naïve enough to think that married men didn't flirt with other women? No, she wasn't that naïve, just ever hopeful that it wasn't true.

With another sigh, and feeling extremely awkward because she'd obviously been foisted on them when they hadn't wanted her to be foisted, she decided not to unpack, just take out the things she would need for the night. Taking out Gwendoline Bear, who went with her everywhere, she sat her in the middle of the bed so that she could see what was going on. Then, after a moment's thought, she also removed the package she'd brought with her, and carefully stowed it in the drawer of the bedside table. It wouldn't do to lose that, not after she'd come all this way to deliver it, and whether she stayed here or not, tomorrow she would begin her enquiries.

Feeling grubby, and, she had to admit, starving hungry, and not at all liking the idea of hiding in her room with only a rumbling tummy for company, she had a quick wash, then changed into clean clothes. Perhaps they would let her make herself a sandwich ... Eyeing Gwen Bear, she wondered if she ought to take her down for company, then gave an enchanting little giggle. They'd think her mad—which she probably was. Still smiling to herself, she ventured downstairs. Not sure where to go, or even if she was supposed to be wandering around, she followed the sound of voices to a room at the back of the house. Standing awkwardly in the doorway of what was obviously the family room, and for the moment unnoticed by the three people present, she stared round her. There was a mishmash of furniture, sofas, rugs, and it all looked enviably comfortable. A shaggy wolfhound lay on a rug before the enormous fireplace, nose on his paws. He opened one eye, glanced at her, then, obviously satisfied that she presented no threat, went back to sleep.

By now, of course, they'd all become aware of her, and conversation stopped. Lowering her lashes, she peeped at Feargal, then gave one of her small smiles. 'I wasn't sure if I was supposed to be wandering round, and I was going to bring Gwendoline Bear with me for company, but she doesn't like strangers, so I came by myself.'

'Could you not have told her that we aren't strangers?' he asked softly.

'Well, yes, but she doesn't always believe me.'

'Ah, full of insecurities, is she? I believe bears are often that way.'

Her eyes full of appreciative laughter, grateful for his understanding, she continued to stare at him. Despite his casual dress of jeans and shirt, there was still an air of sophistication about him that was in sharp variance to those around him, and she cursed Donal again for his stupid sense of humour because it now put her in the most ridiculous position. Although he would probably think that very funny too.

'Meet the family,' Feargal eventually invited when the silence had gone on longer than Ellie felt comfortable with. Raising a languid hand towards a grey-haired woman seated in an armchair beside the dog, and who looked as though she might patronise just the same sort of charity shops as Ellie herself, he introduced, 'My mother.'

She looked vague, but Ellie gave her a little nod anyway. 'My sister Thérèse,' he went on, pointing towards the young dark-haired woman who seemed to be compiling what looked like a list of something or other.

'Hello, Ellie,' she greeted with a broad grin. 'Call me Terry, and I do *wish* you'd brought Gwen Bear with you because this is the most interesting conversation we've had in weeks!'

Returning her smile, and feeling extraordinarily comforted, Ellie hastily returned her attention to Feargal.

'And this heap of fur taking up the warmest spot is Blue. He's quite—amiable,' he said.

'Oh, good.'

'There are two maids, both equally useless. Sisters. Mary and Rose. And rather than alleviating any muddle we might get into they generally add to it. I have a younger brother, Huw, who might or might not put in an appearance with resident girlfriend in tow. I have another sister, Phena, who I hope will *not* put in an appearance, but I'm not entirely confident of the fact.'

'Feargal!' his mother reproved.

Feargal looked unrepentant. 'And should you wish to play tourist, then on the hall table you will find all sorts of literature on things to see and do in the area. Help yourself to anything you want. Mealtimes tend to be a bit vague. The evening meal is usually around seven, although it has been known to be at nine. Breakfast and lunch is usually a question of helping yourself in the kitchen. Anything else you need to know?'

'I don't think so, thank you, and of course I shall only be staying the one night,' she said very firmly.

'Shall you?'

'Yes,' she repeated determinedly in the face of his amused disbelief. 'It's very kind of you to put me up at such short notice, but I really wouldn't dream of imposing. I also forgot to ask how much it would be, and how I should pay...' Feargal's blue eyes were impossibly bland and she found it very hard to keep her face straight. 'The rate for the room, I meant.'

'Ah, we can discuss that later. Anything else?'

'No.' Except I'm starving hungry, and positively yearn for a sandwich.

'That's probably just as well,' Terry giggled, 'because he probably can't think of anything else to tell you.'

'Coats,' his mother said incomprehensibly. At least incomprehensible to Ellie.

'Ah, yes,' Feargal said drily. 'At the back of the house you will find a rummage-room; if you need wellingtons, raincoats, umbrella et cetera, help yourself to whatever fits.'

'Thank you.'

Terry gave a snort of laughter and patted the chair next to her. 'You'll get used to us,' she promised kindly. 'It's nice to see a different face—a very pretty face at that. But hands off Declan; he's my future husband. He'll be by later.'

'Yes. Right.'

Leaning back in her chair, she eyed Ellie with amusement. 'I don't suppose you had time to see much on the way here?'

'No. Oh, well, I made a detour through the Wicklow Mountains—but the hedges were too high to see much, and I had a quick look at the site of the Battle of the Boyne. Did not many people take part?' she asked artlessly.

'Not many people?' Terry echoed with a frown. 'Yes, I think it was a pretty major conflict, wasn't it?' she asked her brother.

'Pretty much,' he agreed drily. 'Why?'

'Because the site that was marked out was so very small. Two people fighting hand to hand would have filled it up!' Ellie said.

Terry burst out laughing, and Feargal gave her a long, thoughtful look, before allowing that little indent to appear beside his mouth again. Really, she was becoming positively enamoured of it!

'I think you will find that the area marked out is intended as a viewing platform in order to see over King William's Glen where the last major military engagement in Ireland was fought,' he instructed quietly. 'Read up on your history, Miss Browne—with an "E".'

Her eyes innocently wide, she gave a slow smile, because she had known it was a viewing platform, of course; and he knew that she knew, which meant that he was teasing her, and that he *was* one of those people who always managed to keep a straight face. His comment also meant that he had been listening to her conversation with the receptionist in Dublin—because he had still been bored? 'I will,' she promised. 'Although I suppose it was against the English,' she observed with a mournful little sigh.

'Weren't everybody's battles?'

Acknowledging the hit, she grinned. 'So which one of our lot instigated this one?'

'William the Third.'

William the Third. That was William of Orange, wasn't it? 'But he wasn't!' she exclaimed in triumph. 'He was Dutch!'

'So he was, in which case we must absolve you from all blame. And if you're really interested in finding out all there is to know about us there's a book on the hall table that records our historic events and heroes, including Francis Ledwidge, our local poet...'

'And Jonathan Swift,' his sister put in.

'And Jonathan Swift,' he acknowledged.

'And did you know that the County of Meath is known as Royal Meath?' Terry put in. 'And that the most powerful kings in pre-Norman Ireland were crowned on the Hill of Tara?'

'No...'

'And then there are the prehistoric tombs of Newgrange, Knowth and Dowth, which you must see, not for the lowly, but royalty. Read *The Burial of King Cormac* by Sir Samuel Ferguson—that's a must for any tourist who argues that Brú na Bóinne—Irish for Newgrange—was a royal burial place. "In Brugh of Boyne shall be his grave, and not in noteless Rosnaree,"' she quoted, then giggled, 'I'm just showing off. It's the spiel we give out to the tourists if they happen to capture one of us when they're wandering round the grounds. It makes us look impressive, which we aren't because we didn't know the half of it either and had to look it all up. Tourists ask the most *extraordinary* questions!'

'Oh,' Ellie said ruefully, 'I'd best try to ask only ordinary questions, then, hadn't I?'

'You had indeed,' Feargal said with an ironic little bow before seating himself in the armchair opposite his mother.

Giving him a doubtful look and a lame smile, she turned back to his sister and asked, 'When are you getting married?'

'Next week.'

'Next week? Oh, perhaps if I'm still in the area I can come and watch.'

'If you're still in the area, you can come to the whole thing!' she grinned. 'You are now, Ellie Browne, cordially invited to my wedding!'

'Well, it's very kind of you,' Ellie mumbled, a bit overwhelmed by the generous offer, 'but I couldn't impose like that—'

'And why on earth not?'

'Because, well, because you don't know me!'

'Sure I do. You're Ellie Browne with an "E".'

With a lame smile, because she wasn't at all sure if Terry was being serious or not, Ellie groaned when her tummy chose that moment to give an embarrassing rumble. 'Sorry,' she muttered.

'Hungry?' Terry asked sympathetically.

'Mm, a bit. Could I make myself a sandwich, do you think?'

'Oh, I think we can run to something a little more substantial than that,' Feargal drawled. Getting lazily to his feet, he went out, and returned a few minutes later to announce, 'There's a snack being laid out for you in the dining-room. This way.'

Getting to her feet, she followed him across the hall and into a room that seemed dark, and faintly depressing, formal. A long, carved oak table dominated the room, heavy chairs to match. With a little grimace, she turned to stare with rather horrified fascination at the dark oil paintings that lined the walls.

'Our illustrious ancestors,' Feargal said softly from close behind her.

'They look as though they're watching me,' she whispered back.

'Indeed they are. They stand in judgement of us all.'

'Oh. They don't look very happy, do they?'

'No. Enjoy your meal.' With another of his faint, elusive smiles, he returned to the lounge—leaving the door open.

Seating herself in solitary splendour, avoiding the accusing glances of his ancestors, she thankfully started on the thick vegetable soup, which, despite Feargal's derogatory remarks about Mary and Rose, was excellent. She could hear everyone's voices quite clearly as she ate, all about someone called Sylvia, who had been truly blessed. Blessed by what, or whom, Ellie wasn't sure.

Finishing up all the fresh crusty bread, she started on the apple pie and cream. Did he still think she had followed him? she wondered. Yes, of course he did, probably thought she and Donal had cooked it up between them. But to actually come and stay in his home! Now that was extraordinary! Almost as though it were meant... Ha, ha, Ellie, let's not get into fantasy here! It was just one of those odd coincidences that happened from time to time. Only how the devil to make him believe that? And why should she care if he didn't? Although she would dearly love to know if it was the norm for women to follow him home!

With one of her quirky smiles, she picked up her coffee. Well, he was certainly very attractive, so she supposed women might. A certain type of woman, anyway. But not her. That wasn't to say she didn't like him, because she did, but then it would be very hard not to! But she doubted it would go any further—well, couldn't go any further as she was only staying the one night. Pity that, because she'd never actually felt this overwhelming tug of attraction before... Had heard about it, read about it, but never actually experienced it, nor this violent awareness, and it would have been nice to see if it led anywhere. She'd never even been in love, she thought wistfully, was beginning to think herself incapable of the emotion, or that her standards were too high—or impossible. She'd *liked* men—of course she had—but for some reason or another it had never deepened into anything else. Not that it was likely to with Feargal, but it might have been fun to enter into a little light flirtation. His particular brand of devastating looks, coupled with bland mockery, was somehow extremely appealing— Although he was probably vain, she comforted herself.

Finishing her coffee, she collected some leaflets from the hall table, and, with the intention of taking them up to her room to read, returned to the lounge to say goodnight—a plan instantly foiled by Feargal's mother, who seemed to have shed her vagueness, along with her daughter, who had disappeared, and patted the seat beside her in silent invitation. As soon as Ellie was seated, she began to rib her gently about her life in England, about how sorry she felt for her living in such a confusing place; regaled her with insights on the local population, and the arrangements being made for the wedding, which was to be held here in the Hall.

'It sounds lovely,' she said warmly, and then, her curiosity getting the better of her, she asked with a teasing smile, 'Why was Sylvia truly blessed?'

'You know her?' Feargal's mother exclaimed in surprise.

'No,' Ellie confessed with a laugh. 'I'm afraid I overheard you talking.'

'Oh.' Her brown eyes creased with amusement, Feargal's mother explained, 'Because she's just had twins.'

'Oh, yes,' Ellie agreed, 'that covers it perfectly. What a lovely phrase. Truly blessed.'

'It will be talked to death for weeks!' she added with another laugh. 'In a small village, the most minor event is discussed endlessly because nothing very much ever happens, and everyone knows everything about everyone else...' For a moment, a shadow moved in her eyes, as though she was remembering something, and then she gave a little shake of her head as though to throw it off, before continuing lightly, 'It can be very irritating. Although it works both ways. If you're in trouble, or have a problem, everyone pitches in to help. And I expect,' she added with a twinkle, 'that before long they'll all be talking about the little English girl who's staying at the Hall.'

'I'm not little,' Ellie protested lightly, as she had protested very many times before.

'No,' she agreed with a puzzled frown. 'But you look it. I don't know why. When you first came in, I would have said you were small, but when you stood beside Terry you seemed exactly the same height, and she's five feet six. Not small at all. Odd, that.'

'Yes,' Ellie agreed inadequately, 'I probably have little legs or something.' Glancing across at Feargal, who was reading a newspaper, or pretending to, she gave a slight smile. Twenty-four hours ago her life had seemed straightforward and uncomplicated, and now she was staying with a family she didn't know, invited to a wedding where she would know none of the guests—and extraordinarily attracted to a man with blue eyes. Why was it, she wondered, that weird things always happened to her?

With a confused little shake of her head, she began to glance quickly through the leaflet about the Battle of the Boyne. It seemed awfully confusing. Not a straightforward battle between the English and Irish, but all sorts of other factors and people involved. Unable to concentrate on the whys and wherefores, she turned her attention to the booklet entitled *Forthcoming Events*.

'They have a leprechaun hunt!' she suddenly exclaimed in delight. 'Where's Carlingford?'

'North,' Feargal said laconically, proving he hadn't been entirely engrossed in his paper. 'And do I assume from your obvious excitement that you now wish to go?'

'Yes, of course!'

'When is it?' his mother asked.

'The thirtieth— Hey, that's tomorrow! How long would it take me to drive up there?'

'No need,' Feargal said quietly. 'I'll take you.'

'You will?' she asked in astonishment.

'Mm. I have to go up there some time, to find out about the Oyster Festival.'

'Oh. Well, it's very kind of you, but I'm sure I'll be able to find it in the car. I don't want to be a—'

'Nuisance, yes, I know,' he agreed. His blue eyes still fixed on her face, he continued blandly, 'But one should never look for leprechauns alone. And if you should happen to find one of the wee men,' he added, his face unnaturally solemn, 'and you wish to get your hands on his gold, you must never, ever take your eyes off him. Look away, even for half a second, and he'll disappear.'

'Oh, I won't,' she agreed. Not entirely sure if she was being teased or not, because so far as she knew the Irish did indeed take leprechauns very seriously, she gave a weak smile. 'Have you ever seen one?'

Shaking his head, his eyes still serious, he denied, 'Not personally, no, but one Easter Sunday, not so very long ago, a suit of clothes was found on Carlingford Mountain. Beside the suit, on a patch of scorched ground, lay some bones. In the pocket of the suit were four gold sovereigns.'

'And it was a leprechaun suit?'

'Mm.'

'I don't believe you!'

'You don't? But you can see the suit in O'Hare's bar. And in Ballyoonan, some sixty years ago, Jimmy Marley himself caught one. He held him firmly, as his parents had always told him to do, and after a battle of wills, staring at him all the time, the leprechaun began to weaken. Jimmy sensed victory, when suddenly the little man exclaimed, "Warrenpoint is on fire!" And Jimmy, who had two sisters there, turned around. It was a fatal move, of course, because when he turned back the leprechaun had gone.'

Glancing at his mother, who gave her a gentle smile, then back to Feargal, she burst out laughing. 'You're pulling my leg!'

'Indeed he is not,' Feargal's mother protested in her gentle way. 'You'll see, when you go. And the finding of the suit a few years ago was the start of the hunt that they now have every year,' she explained matter-of-factly as though it were the most usual thing in the world. 'They hide a number of stone leprechauns on the mountain,' she continued, 'and a reward is paid for those found. They hope, of course, that other genuine artefacts might be discovered.'

'And have they been?' Ellie queried, fascinated.

'No,' she denied sadly, 'not yet at least.'

'But they're still trying?'

'Oh, yes, and even if you don't go to the hunt it's still a beautiful place to see. Between the Mountains of Mourne and Cooley. Full of history, romance and fable. Now,' she added with a complete change of subject that left Ellie feeling bewildered, 'you mustn't feel awkward or in the way, because we're delighted to have you to stay. It's nice to see a fresh face, and such a delightful one at that,' she added with a warm, gentle smile. 'And with such a wicked sense of humour! And don't be feeling that you have to stay in with the family. Come and go as you please, Ellie. You'll be wanting to see as much as you can while you're here, so just use the place as your own. And now I think I'll go to bed.' With another warm smile at Ellie, she added, *'Oiche Mhaith Dhuit.'*

'E ha y gitch?' Ellie queried, trying to copy the strange sounds that Feargal's mother had made.

'It means good night,' Feargal explained as he got to his feet to kiss his mother goodnight.

'Oh, well, I think I'd just better say it in English. Goodnight—and thank you.'

'For what, child?'

'Letting me stay.'

When she'd gone, Ellie glanced at Feargal and wanted to smack him for his slow, knowing smile.

'Two nights?' he asked softly.

'Two,' she agreed, borrowing some of his blandness. Collecting up her leaflets, she made her way up to bed, and gave in to the little grin that had been trying to break out a few minutes before.

Hands linked behind her head, she lay for a while thinking over the extraordinary events of the day. Two days, she thought sleepily. A lot could happen in two days. And with the thought of spending a whole day in his company she gave a contented little smile and snuggled under the duvet. But why had he invited her? That was the puzzle. And she really must remember to ask him what the rate was.

The next morning, without seeing any of the family, who were heaven knew where, she made herself some breakfast under the smiling gaze of Rose or Mary—she didn't know which—and before she could get into a worry as to whether Feargal had meant his offer to take her to Carlingford he walked in through the back door.

'All ready?' he asked with a faint smile.

'Yes. Are you sure you don't mind?'

'If I'd minded, I wouldn't have offered. You will find, Ellie, that I never do anything I don't want to.'

Don't you? she wondered. Did that make life easier? If it did, perhaps she ought to try it herself. He looked clean and fresh and healthy, she thought as she watched him fetch himself a cup of tea, then stand, his hips propped against the table, while he drank it. Confident, competent, and totally in command of himself. So why had he invited her out for the day? Curiosity?

'Is Gwen Bear coming?' he asked with a perfectly straight face.

Shaking her head, her eyes full of laughter, she explained solemnly, 'She has a tummy upset. Too much chocolate yesterday.'

'Ah. Poor Gwen. Ready?'

'Yes, of course.' Smiling her thanks at Mary—or Rose—she quickly got up and followed him. She would take things as they came and not worry about motives, she decided. All very easy to say, but human nature being what it was, and her own curiosity playing a very large part of it, not so easy to do.

CHAPTER THREE

THEY ARRIVED in Carlingford to a fine drizzle, and just
in time for Ellie to take part in the leprechaun hunt.
Feargal bought her ticket, made sure she understood the
map of which part of the mountain was hers to search,
and then pointed her in the right direction.

'Every leprechaun has a price on his head,' he explained with his customary solemnity. 'A hundred
pounds. You'll be all right? Yes, of course you will,' he
answered himself. Lowering his eyes, he stared in some
bemusement at the men's over-large dungarees she was
wearing. The legs were too wide and were chopped off
at least three inches above her boots. 'You look like a
farm labourer off to stack the hay— A very beautiful
farm labourer,' he added softly. 'Put your slicker on;
you'll get soaked. Go on,' he persuaded, 'off you go.
I'll see you back here in the village hotel.'

With a grin, she turned to follow the noisy, laughing, chattering group up the mountain, and in no time
at all had found herself several chums. People very
kindly took her under their wing, explained the rules,
explained the dangers of unexpected holes, and then
encouraged her to spend the next few hours crawling
into and under wet gorse bushes. Giggling like a child,
rueful self-mockery etched on every line of her face, she
applauded when a shout went up, joined in the disappointed groans when it proved a false alarm, commis-

erated with a rather determined little girl who had wandered into her own area of search and who thought she should have found one by *now,* and, thoroughly amused, by herself as much as by others, she whole-heartedly entered into the spirit of the thing.

Reduced to helpless laughter when the young man a few yards away fell headlong into a gulley, forgetting to look where she was putting her own feet, she trod on something hard—and, to her utter astonishment, found a leprechaun. Holding the tiny china figure in her hand, oblivious of the rain sleeting down, she grinned—and then caught sight of the little girl who had been so determined to find one. She looked devastated.

Without even really thinking about it, she pretended to trip, staggered in her direction, deliberately lost her balance, and managed to lob the leprechaun into a clump of grass where the little girl would be able to find it easily.

Wide grey eyes stared at her, glanced at the clump of grass, dithered, mentally debated—and pounced. She half held it out to Ellie as fair play so obviously fought with desire—and Ellie took the decision out of her hands by shouting, 'She's found one!' Scooping the little girl up, she held her high to a scattering of applause.

'It's yours...'

'Nonsense! Wasn't I told you have to hold them tight and not for a minute take your eyes off them? I lost it, you found it, so it's yours.' Lowering the little girl to the ground, she took her hand. 'Hold him very tight now and we'll walk back to the hotel so that you can claim your prize.'

'You don't want to look for another?'

'No,' Ellie denied. 'You don't get lucky twice. They know I'm here now; they won't let me see them again.'

'The real ones?' she whispered.

'Mm.'

Quite glad to abandon what was turning out to be a very wet hunt, she walked with the little girl back to the hotel. And Feargal.

In obvious good humour, she was commiserated with, patted on the back, thanked by the little girl's father, offered half the prize money, which she refused, and looked around for Feargal. He was standing in the corner, talking to some men, and she was able to view him unobserved for a few moments. He really was the most devastating-looking man—tall, confident, charismatic. People automatically seemed to defer to his judgement—or that was the impression she gained. A natural leader of men, well liked, respected, and, as though aware of her watching, he slowly turned his head. His smile was slow, amused. He said something to the men, walked over to the bar, collected a steaming mug and brought it across to her. 'Enjoy yourself?'

'Mm, I always enjoy myself.' Wrapping her palms round the hot coffee, she sipped. Little rivulets of water were running down her neck, and she gave a long shiver when, with a gentle finger, he halted their progress.

'And didn't we all know you for a darling girl?' he whispered in her ear as his fingers continued to blaze fire across her exposed nape.

'And didn't we all know you kissed the blarney stone?' she whispered back. Peeping up at him, she just as quickly looked away when she saw the devilry in his eyes. A calculating sort of devilry?

'I wonder who you truly are?' he queried in the same soft voice that proved that her thoughts had been correct. 'And what you really want. Saint or sinner,' he mused. 'Innocent or guilty.'

'Innocent or guilty of what? Following you?' With a smile as slow as his own, she murmured, 'You won't believe it, I know, but I truly didn't.' Still staring at him, she became distracted by the dark hair that curled damply across his forehead, at the almost delicate arch of his eyebrows, the aquiline nose, the beautiful mouth, and then back to the bright, amused mockery in his blue, blue eyes. It was unfair for one man to be so attractive. So appealing. Aware that she had been staring at him for rather a long time, she blinked and asked hastily, 'Did you sort out your business?'

'I did. We'll have some lunch, and then would you like to have a look round the village?' He made it sound as though it was the most wonderful thing in the world.

'Please,' she said huskily. Don't lose your head, Ellie, she warned herself. He's playing games. You know it, and he thinks you're playing the same one. With a mental grimace, she tucked her hand companionably into his arm, and went to have lunch.

The rain was still drifting across the distant mountain range when they left the hotel, blurring their outlines, obscuring the lough. Taking her hand warmly in his and tucking it into his pocket, he ordered softly, 'Tell me about Elinor Browne with an "E".'

'Not much to tell,' she confessed, her voice as soft as his because talking seemed an intrusion, as though it might break the spell of enchantment she felt wrapped in. Foolish, she knew; perhaps it had something to do with the leprechauns.

'Then tell me how long it is since you left school,' he asked with a fascinatingly wry little smile.

Glancing at him, her eyes filled with amusement, she queried, 'School, or university?'

Coming to a halt, he exclaimed in astonishment, 'University? You never went to university! You don't look old enough to have left senior school!'

'I know,' she agreed with one of her tiny smiles.

'Just how old *are* you, Ellie?'

'Twenty-five.'

'Twenty-five,' he repeated softly. 'Old enough to play.' And, as though that somehow amused him, he continued, 'And what did you take?'

'English.'

'Graduate?'

'Mm.'

'A First?'

'No,' she denied ruefully. 'Second.'

'And what do you want to do with your life?'

'Save things,' she said simply. 'Whales, dolphins, forests...'

'Mm. About time someone did— And here we have the remains of King John's Castle.'

'Our King John?' she asked in surprise as she stared at the ruined fort that overlooked the lough.

'Mm. He apparently visited Carlingford, or more correctly Cathair Linn, as it was called, for three days. He is said to have instructed that a castle be built to impress and intimidate the wild Ui Meith who lived in the surrounding countryside.'

'Heavens, we stick our nose in everywhere, don't we?'

'Not only you,' he laughed. 'We had the Norse and the Danes as well.'

Removing his hand from his pocket, but leaving hers in place, he put his arm round her shoulders and hugged her to his side. The warm weight was a comfort and a delight, and she wondered what he would say if he knew. Look amused, she suspected as they crunched up the crumbling steps, peered through a railing, and then retreated back to the small quay. 'It's a grand sight on a fine day,' he observed quietly as they stared out over the grey water. 'From the top of the hill, with the sun shining across the lough, the mountains standing sharp and clear, it's truly beautiful.'

'Yes,' she agreed, because even on a grey day, with mountains and lough obscured, it was beautiful.

Turning their backs on the dripping stones, Feargal's arm still warmly round her, they walked to view what was left of Taffe's Castle—half a brick wall. The Mint—a whole brick wall, several churches, the remains of Carlingford Abbey—by which time the rain was back in earnest. Urging her into a fast walk, he hurried her across a courtyard and into the craft shop.

'Wait here in the dry and I'll go and bring the car round.'

'All right,' she agreed. His hair, longer than her own, was dripping down his face and neck, and she gave a little smile. 'You're awfully wet.'

'And you aren't?' Trailing his fingers across her wet cheek, capturing the water like tears, he stared down into her eyes. With an odd sigh, and a funny little shake of his head, he turned and hurried out. He dashed across the puddles in the courtyard, lithe and athletic. An altogether devastating man. But why the funny shake of his head? With an unconscious sigh of her own, she touched her fingers to her cheek, just as he had done. Light flirtation? Feelings were beginning to creep in, and that would be monumentally stupid, to actually begin to care for him. Only how the hell did you stop them? It was not a problem that had ever occurred before, and although Ellie knew she was probably playing with fire she was intrigued to know how it would all turn out.

Turning, she smiled at the young woman at the counter. 'Is this a soft day?' she asked whimsically.

'No,' she laughed, 'it's a bloody awful day! And you were the kind lady who gave little Afgie the leprechaun,' she added with a warm smile.

'Good heavens!' Ellie exclaimed to cover her embarrassment. 'News surely does travel fast!'

'Yes, good and bad, both the same, and sure isn't it a wretched day for anything? That was Feargal you were with? You're good friends?'

'New friends,' she corrected. 'You know him?'

'Sure and doesn't every female know the best-looking man in all Ireland?' she laughed.

So it would seem. And, not quite sure how to take that, Ellie hastily looked down at the quilt the woman was folding. 'That's beautiful. Did you make it yourself?'

'For my sins.'

'And the others?'

'Not all; I run a quilting group, and these are some of theirs.'

'They're beautiful. I expect they're very expensive,' she said wistfully.

'I'm afraid so. There's such a lot of work goes into them. The cushions are cheaper.'

Looking round her at the cushions, Ellie spotted one with a Regency man and woman on it. It was beautifully done—and would make a nice present, she decided. She would need to buy something for Terry—even if she didn't stay for the wedding. Discreetly looking at the price, and mentally reviewing how much money she had on her, and thinking wryly that perhaps, after all, she should have accepted half the prize money for the leprechaun, she bought it. When Feargal tooted his car horn, she said her farewells and went out to join him.

'Been spending your money, Ellie?' he asked with his customary mocking smile. Taking the parcel from her, he put it on the back seat.

'It's a quilted cushion,' she explained. 'I thought it would make a nice wedding present for Terry.'

'You intend to stay around for it, then?'

'Not necessarily,' she demurred, 'but she was kind, and I thought I would like to buy her a wedding present—and because you kindly took me in when you didn't want to,' she tacked on softly.

'Who said I didn't want to?'

'It didn't need to be said. It's quite obvious you don't normally take in paying guests.'

His eyes impossibly innocent, he asked, 'And are you going to pay?'

'Oh, yes,' she admitted simply, 'I always pay my debts.'

'Well, there's a bonus. So now tell me the truth.'

'I already did. And if you think about it logically you must know I couldn't have followed you. I left Dublin a long time after you...'

'How do you know?'

Exasperated, she said, 'I don't. Not literally. I just assumed you'd left in the morning. And even if you didn't, *I* didn't know that! And if I didn't follow your

car, which I didn't, how on earth would I have known
where you lived?'

'Donal?' he prompted.

'Donal? Why on earth would Donal tell me where
you lived?'

'Because you asked?'

'No.'

'You didn't ask about me?'

'No—well, yes,' she confessed with a little grin. 'But
that's normal, isn't it? And if anyone should be accused of following anybody it's you! You were the one
who followed me from the ferry!'

'Mm. Although that was . . .'

'Because of boredom—yes, I know,' she agreed in
amusement. 'But that wasn't why *I* came to Slane.'

'You weren't bored?' he asked blandly.

With a little splutter of laughter, she lightly punched
his arm. 'No! And stop talking in circles!'

'Very well, then, if you didn't come because of me,
why did you come to Slane? It's hardly the Mecca of the
Irish countryside. It's a small, ordinary little village, its
only claim to fame the castle, and the burial mounds.
And the battle, of course. A student of history, are you,
Ellie?'

'No,' she denied drily, and he would have to make of
that what he would, because she couldn't explain why
she had come, not the real reason, because it was private, and because the woman she had come to find, the
woman her grandfather had asked her to look up, deliver the package to, might be very angry—and right-
fully so—if she discussed her business with other
people. 'But that still doesn't mean I came because of
you. Because I didn't know you lived here.' But he
didn't believe her; she could see he didn't. 'Happens

often, does it?' she asked with her gentle smile. 'Women following you home?'

'Mm.' Amusement glittering in his beautiful eyes, he added, 'Although anyone who gives away a leprechaun can't be all bad. Can they?' Reaching out, he touched a gentle finger against her lip. 'It was a nice thing to do.'

With an embarrassed shrug, she leaned more comfortably against the seat, and, watching him for a few moments, asked curiously, 'Why did you invite me today?'

'Curiosity.'

'Of what?'

'Your technique.'

'Technique?' Amused query in her eyes, she indicated for him to go on.

'I have been slightly, and I emphasise the slightly, intrigued to know how you would proceed with your seduction.'

'Of you?'

'Mm-hm.'

Her smile widening, she queried, 'You really do think that's why I followed you?'

'Of course.'

'Bit arrogant, isn't it?'

A wicked light dancing in his eyes, he shook his head. 'Women seem to find me—irresistible.'

Her lips twitching, she asked, 'And you can't understand why?'

'Oh, I understand why,' he told her blandly. 'I'm a very wealthy man.'

With a gurgle of laughter, she gave a little nod of acknowledgement. 'All wealthy men have this problem, do they? Even if they look like toads?'

'Mm, toads have been known to turn into princes, haven't they?'

'That's frogs, although I understand the analogy. You think wealth automatically transforms the ugly into the beautiful?'

'Doesn't it?' he asked with a trace of cynicism.

'And you such an antidote to the opposite sex,' she agreed. 'You could give all your money away,' she encouraged, 'and then you wouldn't be pursued at all, would you? And as for my technique—well, my friend, loath as I am to admit it, I don't think I have one.'

'You rely on your natural charm and beauty? Mm, well, I suppose that might be enough, because even with my knowledge of you...'

'Supposed knowledge,' she corrected.

'Knowledge,' he insisted lightly, 'I have to confess that I still find you an unusual and delightful companion—an astonishingly beautiful young woman; and while I watched you in Wexford market I felt—drawn. And the more I get to know you, the more drawn I feel. You look little and lost, are funny and sweet—and I keep getting the overwhelming feeling that I want to take care of you. And I just wish you knew how funny that was,' he added with a quirky smile. 'But don't be weaving fantasies about me, Ellie, about what I might or might not be, will you? Just because I'm being...'

'Amiable?' she put in helpfully.

'Mm, because that would be foolish beyond belief. I don't manipulate easily. And I don't—ever—do anything on impulse.'

'Unless you're bored, of course.'

His smile widening, he acknowledged the hit. 'Unless I'm bored, of course—and I have to admit, in the light of recent developments, that it was a singularly

foolish thing to do. However, there's no harm done.
You do understand what I'm saying, don't you?'

'Oh, yes, Feargal, I understand very well. But, for the
very last time, I did not follow you to Slane. Ask Donal
if you don't believe me.' And, although she was irri-
tated by his refusal to believe her, against her will she
was still mesmerised by the blue eyes that stared so in-
tently into her own, felt warmth steal through her when
he glanced at her mouth. His black lashes were thick
and long, his skin warm, and she wanted to touch and
be touched.

Without the engine running, the interior of the car
was beginning to mist up; condensation lay like rain-
drops on the inside of the windows, and his breath was
warm on her mouth as he murmured, 'Not that I'm
averse, you understand; on the contrary, a little light
dalliance could be a delight.'

'Dalliance?'

'Mm, but do remember that I don't snare easily,
won't you?'

'If at all?'

'Mm.'

'And it's absolutely no good my protesting my innocence?'

'Nope.'

'Then I shan't. Not because I'm not, but because I do
so hate to waste my time. Especially on a lost cause.'

'You disappoint me, Ellie,' he breathed softly, his
eyes still on her mouth. 'It could have been—fun.'

'It still can,' she purred.

His chuckle was rich, and his eyes creased in amusement as he narrowed the last little gap between them.
The touch of his lips on hers was gentle, slow, deliberate, and she gave a little sigh of satisfaction. The most

attractive man in all Ireland, the girl in the shop had said, and perhaps he was. Certainly she found him so, despite what he so obviously thought of her, and as the kiss deepened she felt sleepy and warm and pliant—the nicest thing ever to have happened—and then bereft when he broke the gentle exploration. And how many other women had he made feel like that? Quite a few, she would guess.

'What a pity you didn't allow me to make my own running,' he observed softly. 'Because I was intending to—and who knows where it might have led?'

'Who indeed?' she asked, not believing him for a minute, 'But rather arrogant of you to assume I would be willing to be caught.'

The amusement in his eyes deepened. 'You think I don't know when a woman is interested, Ellie? Oh, I do; believe me, I do.'

Yes, I just bet you do. And did that account for the cynicism and boredom—this constant interest by women? Her amusement matching his, she murmured, 'I never denied the interest, only the pursuit.' And if some malicious god hadn't decreed it was Slane she had to go to, or Slane where he lived, things might have been very different.

'So you did, and in that case, if you're a very good girl, I might yet make love to you.'

'Oh, wow! Thank you so much,' she retorted in mock-gratitude. 'But did it not occur to that massive conceit of yours that I might not want to make love to *you*?'

'No,' he denied with his quirky smile.

Not quite sure whether she wanted to hit him, or laugh, she chose the latter. 'Amiability masking steel?' she pondered aloud. 'But perhaps you're in danger of forgetting that it always did, and always will, take two to tango.'

'You think I might need reminding?' he asked with his slow grin. 'No, Ellie, I don't need reminding at all.'

No; that she did believe.

As though he knew very well what she was thinking, his grin widened, and he burst out laughing. And even his blasted laugh was attractive. Infectious. 'And if we remain stationary much longer the whole village will have it as fact. Married off and with a couple of babies to boot. And the terrible thing is, the thought doesn't fill me with horror at all.' His face still creased in amusement, he turned on the engine and set the demister working. 'Home, Ellie, before I'm snared past retrieving.'

And if she believed that she'd believe anything! Staring from the window, her mouth curved in a smile, she wondered what he would say if she told him that if he did make love to her he would be the first. Laugh, probably, and not believe her. But a little sparring? A light flirtation? With no one getting hurt? Why not? Except that there was the very disturbing thought lodged somewhere in her mind that she didn't want it to be harmless. Or a flirtation. And if he continued to think she had followed him—well, what did it matter? Except that she didn't like being fuel for his amusement. Well, who would? Trouble was, the wretched man was very difficult to dislike.

'And I didn't even get to see a real leprechaun,' she murmured aggrievedly.

'No, but maybe they saw you. And who knows? Perhaps we'll come again.'

'Perhaps.' Although that might be a bit like confronting a tiger and hoping it wouldn't bite. She'd known him barely two days, and already he'd steered her through more emotions than she'd known herself capable of— And, much to her very great surprise, over the next few days he insisted on showing her the countryside. Why? More amusement? Boredom? Not sure she even cared what his motives were, she accompanied him quite happily. Her emotions weren't really engaged. How could they be after knowing him such a short time? And he was a delightful companion, so why not enjoy herself? Pushing aside her need to find Grandfather's friend, unconsciously adopting the philosophy of the Irish that there was always plenty of time, she allowed Feargal to monopolise her—although when he found time to run his farm was anyone's guess. And when she asked he merely gave his quirky smile.

He showed her over the nearby castle, took her for long drives, and on the last day of his—as he called it— 'snatched holiday', seemingly relaxed and happy to be playing truant from the demands of his busy life, he drove to Bettystown. Parking in the little car park opposite the fairground, closed and deserted now, with covers hiding the rides, they walked hand in hand down to the beach. It stretched for miles in each direction, with not a soul to be seen. Golden sand and blue sea, and in the clear blue sky a promise of summer. With a contented sigh, she exclaimed, 'It's beautiful!'

'Yes. Seeing it like this, it's hard to imagine it packed with bodies, as it is at weekends when the weather's good. Want to walk for a bit?'

'OK.'

They wandered silently for what seemed like miles, both wrapped in their own thoughts, and the only person they saw was a red-jumpered golfer on the course behind the beach. He waved at them and Ellie smiled.

'That would never happen at home. Everyone here is so friendly. Everyone says hello.'

'Yes, especially to Ellie Browne, who would bring a smile to the gloomiest face.' Halting, he released her hand and framed her exquisite face with warm palms. His beautiful eyes were full of warmth and laughter, and if there was also a trace of cynicism she chose not to identify it. 'Decided to tell the truth yet?'

Exasperated, she moved slightly away. 'I already told you the truth.'

'I wonder?' he murmured thoughtfully. 'Certainly, so far, you've made no attempt to consolidate your position.'

'What position?'

'This position.' Without warning, he pulled her into his arms. 'This oh, so delightful, intimate position.' His eyes crinkled with laughter, he stared down into her lovely face. 'Or are you still biding your time?'

'Oh, biding my time, I expect,' she retorted, she had to admit, slightly breathlessly. Although that was natural, wasn't it? He had a terrific body—and it seemed to match hers to perfection.

Lowering his head, he captured her mouth, expertly learned all there was to know about Ellie Browne's responses—all about how putty felt when it was thoroughly warmed. He kissed her with an expertise that was outside her experience, with a knowledge that was never learned from any book, and, much to her surprise, she felt a stab of jealousy for all those other women who must have stood as she stood now, arms round his strong frame, mouth ravaged by his skill. When he broke the kiss, he still looked amused.

Ellie didn't; she looked dazed, then gave a rueful smile that she prayed masked her disquiet and regret. 'Holiday over?' she guessed.

'I think so. Dalliance at an end. It's been—delightful, and either you are a very good actress or you are genuinely innocent of guile. Which is it, Ellie?'

To admit to being innocent of guile somehow smacked of being undesirable, immature, but far better that than be thought an actress. 'The former,' she admitted with a wry little smile. Shaky, but definitely wry.

'Not an actress?'

'No.'

'So it was just impulse that sent you up here?'

'No, Feargal,' she said with a little sigh, 'it was coincidence. I got the shock of my life when you opened the front door; couldn't you tell?' She waited, hopeful, but his cynicism was back, and she pulled a funny face. 'Boy, you must have had some really bad experiences with women to make you so distrustful.'

'Bad?' he queried blandly. 'No, not bad. Boring. Predictable.' Catching her hand, he began tugging her back towards the car. 'Hungry?'

'A bit, why? Going to buy me dinner?'

'Why not? Reward for being a good girl.'

'That's what I like about you, Feargal,' she said admiringly. 'You can be so damned patronising!'

But if she'd hoped to ruffle his conceit she didn't; he merely laughed. 'You know, if you'd been honest, I think I might have liked you more. There's something quite attractive about a little *ingénue.*'

'Is there?'

'Mm.' Courteously seating her inside the car first, he walked round to the driver's side, and when he had settled himself behind the wheel asked unexpectedly, 'Have you visited one of our pubs yet?'

'No,' she denied.

'Then you should. To travel through Ireland without visiting a pub would be to miss out on a huge chunk of Irish life. It's far more than just a place to drink; it's the social and conversational heart of any Irish village. If you're after food, advice, company, or a good crack, the pub is the place to head for.'

'Crack?' she queried, interested, despite the fact that he sounded like a damned travel guide.

'Chat, gossip,' he explained. 'Talking is an important business here, and drink the great lubricant—are you sulking?'

'No.' And she wasn't. Disappointed maybe, in both him and herself, but not sulking.

'Do you need to go back to the house to change?'

'I'd like to tidy up if I may.'

'Certainly you may,' he parodied, poking fun of her polite response. 'I did warn you, Ellie,' he said more gently.

'So you did.' How to tell him that was not why she was being poky? Yet to say anything at all would only serve to convince him that he was right and she wrong. With a long sigh, she tried to shake off her sombre mood. 'Tell me about those three-storey houses that stand at each corner of the crossroads. Why are they practically identical?'

'Because four sisters are said to have built them.'

'And did they?'

'No,' he laughed, 'but it makes a good tale.' Drawing up outside the house, he urged her inside. 'Five minutes, Ellie; I'll meet you back here.'

With a little nod, she hurried inside and up to her room. Five minutes later, without giving herself time to think, be disappointed that she probably wouldn't see him again after today, she ran lightly down the stairs and out through the front door. Feargal was there before her, and she halted for a moment to watch him. He was leaning against the car, staring rather broodingly at the rhododendrons. He looked remote, and somehow weary. Trouble on the farm? With his horses? Before she could pursue her thoughts further, he lifted his head, and with a slight smile straightened to face her.

'You forgot to brush your hair,' he observed solemnly.

'No I didn— Oh!' she exclaimed with a laugh that even to herself sounded slightly false. 'I almost took you seriously for a minute. And I did brush it.'

'You did? How does one tell?' Catching her hand, he tucked it into his arm and they walked slowly down into the village. Last time to touch him, last time to enjoy his banter. And trust you to like the one person you can never have, she mused.

Halting outside the pub, Ellie lingered to read the chalked sign outside. Or try to read it. She found it very difficult to get her tongue round the unfamiliar words. 'What does that mean?'

'*Ceol tradistiunta?* Traditional music.'

'Oh!' she exclaimed, pleased. 'Fiddles and things?'

'Yes, Ellie,' he agreed drily, 'fiddles and things.'

He was obviously well-known because people nodded to him, smiled, glanced curiously at her as Feargal sat her at a small table at the rear.

'Can't we sit at the front? Isn't that where the music is to be?'

'No, we can't, and yes, it is,' he smiled. 'The empty seats are reserved for people who might want to join in. Unless you do?' he asked lightly.

'Good lord, no! If I sang, I'd clear the pub in seconds!'

With a faint smile, he asked, 'What would you like to drink?'

'Vodka and lemonade?'

'Sure. To eat?'

'Oh, anything—er—so long as it's vegetarian. A salad maybe?' To be honest, she was no longer very hungry.

'Fine.'

While he went up to the bar to order, Ellie settled back in her seat, and, with a rather sad light in her eyes, watched him. It was conceivable, she supposed, that if she remained in the village she might see him from time to time, and if she was lucky, she thought bleakly, he might even speak to her.

'*Dia duit.*'

Jeea ditch? Swinging round in surprise, she looked at the elderly man who had spoken. He was smiling at her, his brown eyes twinkling with amusement.

With a hesitant smile back, and a funny little grimace, she apologized, 'I'm sorry, I don't know what that means.'

'It means hello.'

'Oh. Jeea ditch,' she mumbled, not at all sure she had pronounced it right.

'No, no,' he grinned. 'You say in return, *Diás muire duit.*'

'Oh, jeea smoora ditch,' she repeated obediently.

'Very good,' he complimented. 'You're on holiday? From England?'

'Yes.'

'And what do you think?'

'I think it's all splendid,' she smiled. 'Not at all like England.'

'No, not at all,' he agreed with another twinkle. 'And you've come to listen to the *sean nós?*'

'I don't know. Have I?'

'Certainly.'

With an infectious laugh, she confessed, 'I don't know what that is, either.'

'A style of singing,' Feargal said from beside her. Nodding to the elderly man, who smiled and turned back to his own companion, he handed Ellie her drink, and sat beside her with his own pint. 'The singer is not allowed to sing any two verses of a song in the same way. In fact some songs have only two lines,' he explained.

A doubtful smile in her eyes, she reproved softly, 'I never know if you're teasing me or not.'

'On this occasion not. Your salad will be here in a few moments.'

'Thank you.' Not knowing what else to say, she looked back towards the stage area in time to see a man with a fiddle emerge from a side-room, and all conversation magically hushed.

'Is a fiddle the same as a violin?' she whispered.

'Yes, it differs only in the way it's played.'

'Oh,' she murmured inadequately. Sipping her drink, she settled down to be quiet, and tried very hard not to be so aware of Feargal so close beside her. Did he too regret the ending of their friendship? No, that was silly; why should he be? He'd been merely indulging in an amusing diversion to pass the time. So had she, initially, only she had the horrible feeling that somewhere along the way she had begun to like him too much. Out of all the boys—men—she had known, not one had made her feel like this; so unsettled, so wanting, so— happy. If she stretched out her hand just the tiniest bit, she would be able to touch his where it rested on his knee. A strong hand, long-fingered, brown. And if she leaned sideways just a fraction her shoulder would touch his. She wanted to be held by him, and as the sad, poignant music began it set up a yearning inside of her that she didn't know how to dispel. Was this how people felt when they fell in love? She had no idea, no experience to draw on. With a faint, elusive smile, she recalled a similar sort of feeling when she had yearned after the paperboy when she'd been fourteen. But since then? Nothing. No spark, no enjoyable crossing of swords with someone, no delight in teasing—and yet, really, she knew him not at all. He only let her see what he wanted her to see, gave no hint of what he was really like, not the man inside. What did he want from his life—if anything?

When the musician finished, to thunderous applause, and before the singing started, her salad was brought. 'Aren't you eating?' she whispered.

'No, I'm not hungry.' With one of his faint smiles, he indicated for her to eat.

Exactly as I appear is exactly as I am, he had said that day in Carlingford. What a long time ago that seemed now, and how sure she had been that he would not be able to disrupt her feelings. And she hadn't honestly thought he had—until just a few hours ago on the beach when he'd said that this was goodbye. Thankful that in the dim bar her confusion would not be evident, she focused all her attention on her meal, and found it very, very hard to swallow.

The singing seemed equally sad, and as the evening progressed she began to feel more and more melancholy. Normally such a happy, sunny person, she felt a vague disquiet, as though she was changing without her wanting to. She was really quite glad when the evening ended.

It was dark when they got outside, and, walking silently beside him, she stared up at the stars, and gave an unconscious little sigh.

'Feeling sad, Ellie?'

'Mm.'

'Yes, it can have that effect. Tell me about your home. What you do there.'

'I don't do anything much,' she confessed quietly. 'I can't seem to find a job. In fact none of my year from university has a job,' she said despondently.

'Not only in England.'

'No. It's a bit of a catch twenty-two. Employers want people with experience, only how do you get experience if you can't get a job?'

'You live at home with your parents?'

'No,' she denied with a tiny smile. 'I have a little flat... No, that's not strictly true; it's a room with shared bathroom and kitchen.'

'And how do you afford that?'

'I get housing benefit. Not a lot, but enough to manage on if I'm careful.'

'Your parents don't help out?'

'No,' she said wryly. 'They seem to think I should stand on my own two feet—which is only right and proper,' she added hastily in case he should think she was whingeing. 'And it's better than living at home.'

'Because you don't get on with them?'

'Oh, yes... Well, sort of. Dad and I are quite good friends, but I think I'm a severe disappointment to my mother. I don't seem to be able to do any of the things she wants me to do. Be any of the things she wants me to be.'

'And what is it she wants you to be?'

'Married. Sophisticated. Smart. She looks at me sometimes and gives sad little sighs, bewildered smiles, as though she really isn't quite sure where I come from. But I don't like going to posh functions, trying to make conversation with silly people who have nothing to say. I like being me as I am,' she said simply and rather sadly.

'A gypsy in your soul, hm?'

'I suppose so.'

'And you don't want to get married?' he asked. 'Only play the field?'

'That wasn't a very nice observation to make,' she reproved, 'and, yes, I would like to get married.' Although maybe it might have been better to lie, because that might have convinced him, mightn't it, that she had no designs on him? But she wasn't very good at lying— and, anyway, didn't see why she should. 'I'd like to have lots of little babies too, but not with...'

'A Hooray Henry?' he queried, but not with any real degree of interest. 'Isn't that what you call them?'

'Yes,' she agreed quietly, and suddenly found that there was the most awful lump in her throat, and that her vision was blurred by tears. *I don't want to go home,* she thought. *I want to stay here, where everyone says hello, where one day Feargal might, or might not, believe me.*

'What are you thinking?'

'Oh, nothing, just silly things.' She could hardly tell him how safe she felt with him. How protected.

'And here we are at home,' he observed, almost mockingly, she thought.

'Yes.'

'You'll be leaving tomorrow?' he asked—pointedly.

'Yes.' What else could she say?

'Then I'll say goodbye now.' Turning her to face him, he framed her exquisite face with his strong palms. 'It might have been different, mightn't it?'

'Yes.'

With a faint smile that showed not a hint of regret, he brushed his mouth against hers. 'Take care, Ellie. Don't go following any more men home, will you? They might not be as . . .'

'Amiable?' she asked tartly.

'Mm.' Ushering her inside, he walked into his study and just as he was about to close the door she remembered she hadn't settled up with him.

'Feargal? You forgot to tell me how much I owe.'

Turning, he stared at her for a moment, before replying, almost curtly, she thought, 'Nothing. I'll put it down to experience.' With a brief nod, as though she were no more than a casual acquaintance, he closed the door. Nothing wrong in his world, and shouldn't be in hers—and she couldn't really understand why it was. Her mental assurances didn't seem to offer much comfort, and she certainly didn't think she wanted to be put down as an experience. She would much rather have paid. With a sigh, for things vaguely wrong with her life, she walked along to the lounge where she found Feargal's mother. She was sitting before the fire, knitting.

'Hello, dear,' she smiled. 'I've barely seen you these last few days. My fault, I know—I've had a few things on my mind. How did the leprechaun hunt go?'

The leprechaun hunt? Heavens, that seemed light-years away. Forcing a smile, she enthused, 'Oh, it was great. I even found one. Not real, of course.'

'No, of course not,' she agreed solemnly. Patting the seat beside her, she commiserated, 'You didn't have the best weather for it.'

'No. The mountains were shrouded in mist and the lough looked grey and uninviting, and I got very wet. What are you knitting?'

With a sideways look, a twinkle in her dark eyes, she confessed, 'I have no idea. I was thinking I might use up all my odd scraps of wool, to make a scarf perhaps, but who would wear such a strange-looking garment?' She held it up, and they both viewed the uneven multicoloured stripes.

'Someone like me?' Ellie offered.

'Then it will be yours!'

'Oh, no, I was only teasing, and I really only came in to tell you that I'm leaving tomorrow, and to thank you for being so kind, and—well, to say goodbye. And I don't even know your name,' she confessed ruefully. 'I've been here nearly a week and I never thought to ask.'

'No, my son has been rather monopolising your company, hasn't he?' she teased. 'It's McMahon.'

'McMahon? But that's the name...' Surely it couldn't be that easy? To come all this way and find herself staying in the house of the people with the same name as those she was trying to trace? No, of course it couldn't. There must be hundreds of people named McMahon— Be ironic, though, wouldn't it, if she'd been staying all this time in the house of the woman she was looking for? Not really believing it, and in total ignorance of the can of worms she was about to open, she asked, 'Are there many with that name in the area?'

'A few; why?'

'Well...' Not quite sure how to broach the subject, and not wishing to be indiscreet, she murmured awkwardly, 'I don't quite know how to put this, but part of the reason for my visit was to try and trace someone who lived here a long time ago, only I don't quite like to ask around, because the person I'm looking for might not like it—might not want everyone to know her business.'

'Well, I've lived here all my married life, and if I promise to be very discreet, not gossip about it...'

Mortified, Ellie exclaimed, 'Oh! I didn't mean to imply...'

'I know, child, I was only teasing. Come on, who is it you're looking for? Someone named McMahon?'

'Yes, at least the lady I was trying to trace married someone called McMahon. Her name was Marie O'Donn—' And she knew. By the way Feargal's mother stared at her, suddenly she knew. 'It was you?' she asked in astonished disbelief.

'Certainly my name was O'Donnell, but why on earth...?'

'It's nothing awful, I promise you,' Ellie reassured her hastily. 'Honestly. If you were Marie O'Donnell, then I have something for you!' Jumping to her feet, she hurried back to her room, collected the package, and hurried back to the lounge. Dragging up a stool, she sat in front of the older woman's legs, and placed the package in her lap. 'I can't believe it's such a coincidence, that I've actually been staying in the house of the

person I came to look for! Hey, don't look so terrified,' she smiled, 'it's only some letters and a little ornament that Gramps thought you might like. He said
you'd always admired it.'

'Gramps?' she frowned.

'Yes, my grandfather. He knew you ages ago, when
you lived in England—David Harland. You worked for
him,' she prompted when Mrs McMahon only continued to stare worriedly at the package.

'David?' she exclaimed faintly. Leaning back in her
chair, she stared at Ellie in shock. 'You're his granddaughter?'

'Yes.'

Searching Ellie's face, perhaps looking for some re-
semblance, she gave a funny little sigh. 'David Harland. After all these years. And don't they say your
troubles will always come home to roost?' Glancing
down at the package as though it might just possibly
bite, she took a deep breath and began to unpick the
sellotape that held it intact. Lifting out the ornament,
a beautifully sculpted ballerina on point, she stared at
it for a moment, then gave a faint, rather sad smile.

'She's beautiful, isn't she?' Ellie said softly.

'Yes. She used to stand on his desk... Lord, Ellie, but
it was a long time ago, and what a green girl I was. Fresh
over from Ireland, and I thought it would be so easy to
find a little office job—typing, filing.' Her eyes unfo-
cused, her mind back in the past, she continued softly,
reminiscently, 'It was after the war, you see, and women
had become used to working, being independent, and
jobs they'd held down while their men were away
fighting they weren't about to give up easily. I'd just
been turned down for yet another job, hardly any

money left—desperate, I was, and out comes your grandfather, asks me what's wrong.'

'And he gave you a job?'

'Yes. Not typing or anything—he said he didn't need a secretary; what he did need, he said, was someone to keep his office nice. Fresh flowers, dust round... It wouldn't be much, but would maybe tide me over till I could find something better. He was a good man.'

'Yes.'

Looking up at Ellie, Mrs McMahon suddenly gave a little start, and, to Ellie's astonishment, she suddenly looked wary. 'What did he say about me?'

'About you?' she asked in bewilderment.

'Yes. What did he tell you?'

'Nothing much,' she said with a little puzzled shake of her head. 'Only that he'd known you, that you might like to have the letters and the statue.'

'Are you sure?'

'Yes, of course.'

'And he just asked you to deliver them?'

'Yes. Why? Are you not pleased to have them?'

'Oh, yes,' she mumbled evasively, 'but Ellie, it might be best not to say anything to...' Raising her eyes, she stared in rather horrified fascination at the opening door. 'Feargal,' she concluded lamely.

'And what must we not say to Feargal?' he asked from the doorway.

'Nothing.' The package was far too large to stuff down the side of the chair, but Mrs McMahon tried anyway, then gave up, and, with a helpless glance at her son, leaned back, 'Nothing,' she repeated. 'Just a little something Ellie brought for me.'

'The statue?' he asked, walking across. Taking it from his mother, he held it on his palm. 'Nice. You have been a busy girl, haven't you? Buying all these thank-you presents.' For some reason, he didn't look very pleased about it.

'It wasn't—' she began, only to be interrupted by Mrs McMahon saying the opposite.

'Yes.'

Looking from one to the other, not exactly suspicious, but certainly puzzled, he glanced at the package. 'And that?'

'Nothing. It's nothing at all! Good heavens, is that the time? I have to be up early tomorrow, so if you'll excuse me I think I'll go up to bed.' Gathering the package firmly in her hands, she jumped to her feet and tried to edge past her son.

Thoroughly bewildered, and wondering why on earth Mrs McMahon was behaving so strangely, Ellie watched Feargal teasingly twitch the package out of his mother's hands. 'Secrets, Mother?'

'No, and give that right back, Feargal McMahon!'

With a faint smile, he was about to do so, when his mother grabbed too soon, and the pile of letters slipped to the floor. He was quicker than his mother in bending to retrieve them—and all his amusement vanished. His blue eyes looked suddenly brighter, sharper, as he read the name printed on the front of one of the letters. 'David Harland?' he queried coldly. 'What the hell are these doing here?'

With a fatalistic air, her shoulders tiredly slumped, Mrs McMahon glanced at Ellie, then back to her son. 'Ellie brought them. She's his granddaughter.'

'His *what?*'

'Granddaughter,' she repeated unnecessarily.

Slowly straightening, the letters held in his hand, he looked at Ellie. 'You brought these?'

'Yes, but . . . And no,' she denied strenuously as she saw which way his mind was working, 'I did not know she lived here!'

'Really?' With a withering glance, he returned his attention to the letters and began to rifle through them.

'Yes, really! And they're for your mother, not you!' she declared, incensed that he should show so little consideration.

'I'm well aware of whom they're for,' he bit out, and Ellie belatedly became rather frighteningly aware of the dangerous quality in him that had only been hinted at before. It was as though a light had gone out somewhere inside of him. Looking hastily away, she stared at his mother. She looked—frightened, and resigned. Why? What was so awful about the letters? So far as she knew they were only the result of an innocent friendship, so why Feargal's anger? His mother's fear? He obviously knew about David Harland, but why did that make him so cross? All right, he now knew why she had come—not to follow him as he'd thought, but to deliver the letters; but that still didn't explain his anger.

'I don't understand what's wrong,' she said quietly. 'They're only letters.'

'Only?' he asked coldly.

'Yes! Did you want to discuss them in private? Should I go away?'

He gave her a look of such hatred that she took an involuntary step backwards. 'What?' she whispered.

'What do you think?' he demanded angrily.

'I don't know,' she denied with a puzzled frown.

'You don't? How extraordinary. Just another coincidence, is it, Ellie?'

'Yes, I just told you! I only knew the name! I didn't know she lived here! There was no address on the letters! Well, look if you don't believe me!' she snapped in exasperation. 'It says only Slane! And I don't in the least understand why you're so angry! They're only some letters that I thought your mother would like to have!'

'Oh, I'm very sure of that,' he agreed with biting derision.

Glancing at his mother, she whispered worriedly, 'What did I do?'

'How did you come by them?' Feargal demanded without allowing his mother to answer.

'Gramps gave them to me.'

'And how much do you want?'

'Want?'

'Yes, want?' he bit out. 'Money, Miss Browne. How—?'

'Feargal!' his mother interrupted, shocked. 'She doesn't wa—'

'How much do you want?' he persisted.

'For what? I don't understand what you're talking about.'

'Such a sweet little face,' he derided, his eyes as cold and flat as glass. 'So tailor-made for blackmail!'

'Blackmail?' she whispered, horrified. 'What blackmail?'

Giving her a look of disgust, he bent forward and flung the whole package on the fire.

'No! For God's sake, Feargal! That won't help!' Reaching out, Mrs McMahon tried frantically to rescue them.

'You actually want to keep them?' he asked with bitter incredulity. 'After all the trouble...'

'Yes, I do! Of course I do! Oh Feargal, please,' she pleaded agitatedly.

With a sound that seemed full of pain and anger and disgust, he picked up the poker and quickly raked them out into the hearth. With his boot, he stamped out the tiny flames before they could grow. Turning on Ellie, he castigated savagely, 'All this week, with your sweet, happy little face, pretending to be something you're not. And today—today when I thought you'd taken to leaving with resignation and humour, you were planning this little surprise. Were these held in reserve in case I wouldn't be duped? So why not give them to me? You've had ample opportunity to do so. Why my mother? What in God's name did she ever do to you?'

'Nothing...'

'No. Nothing! So why try to hurt her?'

'Hurt her? Why would I want to hurt her?' Understanding none of it, Ellie stared from one to the other. 'I don't understand why you're so angry,' she repeated helplessly. 'I thought your mother would like to have them. I thought—'

'You thought it was a wonderful way to get money, revenge,' he contradicted. 'Isn't that why he gave them to you?'

'Gramps? No! He wouldn't do anything like that! He gave them to me just before he died, and asked—'

'He's dead?' Mrs McMahon interrupted with obvious sadness.

'Yes. I'm sorry. He died a few months ago.'

'And I suppose your grandmother, and your parents, and God knows who else has been pawing through them!' Feargal raged.

'No! Of course not! They were given to me! And I certainly didn't show them to anyone else! Gramps asked me if I would come and return them, together with the statue, because he thought your mother would like to have them, and so I did! What did I do that was so wrong?' she wailed. 'Why is everyone so upset? Oh, Mrs McMahon, I'm sorry. I never meant for this to happen! I...' Suddenly realising that she no longer had their attention, and that they were both listening to a woman's voice loudly exclaiming from outside, she lamely tailed off.

'Oh, God!' Feargal exclaimed in disgust. 'Mightn't I have known that she would have such perfect timing?' turning to his mother, he explained, 'That's what I was coming to tell you—that Phena was on her way. That Phena has obviously arrived,' he substituted bitterly. Swinging round on Ellie, he warned, 'You mention one word of this to her, and I'll kill you!'

Stooping, he grabbed up the letters and stuffed them down behind the chair cushion just as the door opened and his sister walked in. She looked little, and soft, and altogether charming, not at all the sort of person you wouldn't want to come and stay as Feargal had once intimated. Her hair was fair, expertly styled to look wind-swept, her make-up discreet, her suit, although clearly expensive, was understated elegance to a T. This was the woman whom Feargal said he hoped wouldn't come?

Hovering just inside the door, she gave them a look of amusement. 'Well, I must say I didn't expect the red carpet, but neither did I expect you all to look at me as though I were the devil incarnate! What's up?'

'Nothing,' both Feargal and his mother said together. Feargal recovered first. 'Sorry,' he apologised without sounding in the least apologetic. 'We were arguing.'

'Again?'

'Yes, Phena, again. Are you staying the night?'

'Yes, brother mine,' she said with a curiously sweet smile. 'I am. If that's all right?'

'Don't play games, Phena, I'm not in the mood! I'll go and tell Rose to make up your room.' Without looking at anyone else, he went out.

'What's up with his lordship?' she asked as she walked across to drop a kiss on her mother's proffered cheek.

'Oh, nothing,' Mrs McMahon said vaguely. 'It's just one of those days.'

'It must be,' she laughed, 'if he's suddenly prepared to run his own errands!'

'Phena,' she said wearily, 'that's enough. Now, you won't have met Ellie,' she added with a tired smile for the younger girl. 'She's been staying with us for a few days.'

Turning to Ellie, Phena smiled. 'Hello, Ellie.'

'Hi,' Ellie mumbled, and before she could get drawn into any more dramas she quickly excused herself. 'You'll have things to talk about, I expect, so I'll say goodnight.' With another mumbled apology, she fled.

CHAPTER FOUR

NOW WAS OBVIOUSLY not the time to confront Feargal
and ask what the devil he'd been talking about. She'd
have to catch him in the morning— But catch him she
would, she vowed silently. Blackmail? Revenge? Walking thoughtfully up to her room, she sat on the bed.
Feeling thoroughly bewildered, hardly able to believe
she had caused so much trouble without even knowing
why, she picked up Gwen Bear and hugged her warm,
furry body to her for comfort. So much for good in-
tentions. Easy to understand how the road to hell came
to be paved with them.

But why had the letters caused so much upset? True,
she'd only glanced through them, hadn't read them
properly, because to do so had seemed like prying; but
they'd seemed innocuous enough, just letters from a
young girl. To her grandfather, admittedly, a man who
must have been old enough to have been her father, but
still surely nothing to get in such a stew over. He'd been
married, of course, and in those days perhaps it had
been frowned upon for a married man to be friendly
with a young girl, but that's all it had been—friendship. And it had all been such a long time ago! Over
forty years! And before Marie O'Donnell had married.
So why the fuss? *Why* had the letters made Feargal so
angry? And why mustn't Phena know anything about
them? Perhaps she could ask Terry. If she ever saw her,

she thought worriedly; she always seemed to be rushing off somewhere—and then she jumped when someone tapped on the door.

'Ellie?'

His voice sounded unbelievably distant, cold, and she was very tempted to ignore it, but if she did that he would come in anyway, she knew that, and she did after all want to talk to him, didn't she? Well, yes, but not with him in this mood. Feeling decidedly wary and unsure of herself, she got up to answer it. There was no warmth in his eyes now, no smile, only blue steel. He looked—formidable. One to be obeyed. 'You'd best come in,' she murmured reluctantly.

'I was intending to.' Moving her to one side, he came in and closed the door.

With a little grimace she walked back towards the bed, and then leaned against one of the posts. She felt somehow safer with something against her back. 'Why are you so angry?' she asked quietly. 'And why on earth should you automatically assume that I came here with the express purpose of blackmail?'

'Why do you think?'

'Feargal!' she exclaimed in exasperation. 'Stop answering questions with questions and tell me what's going on! What, please, is so terrible about bringing a few letters? And why on earth mustn't Phena know about them?'

'We will leave my sister out of this discussion, thank you. And keep your voice down.'

'But why? What is it that Phena mustn't know?' she pleaded.

'Don't play games. You know why.'

'But I don't!' Staring at him worriedly, she slowly sank down to sit on the edge of the bed. 'You really believe that I came here to cause trouble, don't you?'

Leaning back against the door, his arms folded, he just looked at her.

'But why would I do that? It doesn't make sense!'

'What, precisely, did your grandfather tell you about my mother?'

'Nothing specific,' she murmured with a frown of recollection, 'just general things, you know. How pretty she was, how sweet.'

'Oh, I can imagine,' he retorted derisively. 'And your grandmother?'

'Grandmother?' she queried in perplexity. 'Why would Grandmother say anything about her? I don't think she knew her. And even if she did she'd hardly be likely to tell me—it would have been gossip. And Grandmother certainly didn't indulge in that! She always seemed a very cold sort of person.' A trait her own mother seemed to have inherited. Or had she only been cold because she'd known of her husband's friendship with a beautiful young Irish girl? No, that was silly. Or had he had a predilection for liking young ladies? No way to know now.

'She's dead too?' he asked in the same cold, interrogative voice.

'Mm? Oh, yes, some years ago. Her heart, I think.'

'And your grandfather?'

A sad little smile on her mouth, she said softly, 'Just quietly, as he always was, in his sleep.'

'And before he went to this—gentle—sleep,' he derided, 'he asked you to return her letters, bring the statuette, and...?'

'And?' she repeated in bewilderment. 'And what?'

'And what else did he say?'

'Nothing,' she denied, 'or only that he missed her when she returned to Ireland. Feargal, I don't in the least understand what it is you're trying to find out.'

Ignoring her question, he persisted, 'And naturally told you why.'

'Why she returned to Ireland, do you mean?'

'Yes.'

Searching her memory, she finally shook her head. 'No, just that she went back. That they wrote to each other for a while.'

'Wrote to each other for a while,' he echoed with the same derisive twist to his mouth. 'Eighteen, she was, no experience of the world, and hadn't they all told her before she left to go to England what a wicked place it was?' he parodied savagely. 'How the men would take advantage of her?'

'Advantage?'

'Yes. Only of course it wasn't that at all, was it?'

'It wasn't?' Ellie queried. He'd sounded as though he was being sarcastic, or ironic, but again she hadn't a clue what he meant. 'Why wasn't it?'

'And then he had the infernal nerve to write and ask if she was managing all right,' he continued bitingly.

'Managing? Was it hard?' Then, exasperated by her own confusion, and the fact that they seemed to be going round in circles, Ellie demanded, 'Feargal, just tell me what it is you want to know—what, in fact, we're supposed to be talking about!'

'Phena,' he prompted softly.

'Phena? What about Phena? You just said we had to leave her out of the conversation!'

Slamming forward, making her scramble backwards in alarm, he gritted savagely, 'Don't! Don't sit there with your pretty little face all bewildered! Don't you dare sit there and pretend innocence! There was no point bringing the letters if you didn't know about her!'

'Know what about her?' What in God's name were they talking about now? she thought frantically.

'Her parentage! The fact of her being your grandfather's little by-blow!'

'His what?' she queried in astonishment. 'His... Don't be so absurd!' His face darkened, and as he strode grimly towards her she stumbled hastily to her feet and backed up against the wall. Her face alarmed, she held out her arm in a stupid attempt to ward him off. 'Are you seriously trying to tell me that Gramps...that he made your mother pregnant with...?'

Easily knocking her arm to one side, he halted only inches from her. 'Pregnant and delivered,' he rasped vehemently, 'as you very well know. And if you don't keep your voice down I'm very likely to become violent!'

'Become?' she asked in astonishment. 'Become? You *are* violent! And how the Sam Hill could I have known that your mother was...that she...and by Gramps? If it weren't so ludicrous, it would be laughable! And how dare you accuse...?'

'Accuse?' he asked softly, and the few inches separating them narrowed alarmingly.

'Yes, accuse!' she spat nervously. 'Gramps would never—and anyway he couldn't...'

'Couldn't? Are you calling my mother a liar?' he asked with silky menace.

'I'm not calling anyone anything! I'm merely saying that Gramps could not have been the father of her child!' She knew damn well he couldn't! Gramps couldn't have children. Both his son and daughter had been adopted.

'Are you? Then why—?' And then he broke off. Staring at her, a puzzled frown in his eyes, he took a step back.

'Now what?' she demanded. Feeling braver now that he wasn't looming so close, she added, 'Well? What other little maggots have you got running around in that fertile brain of yours?'

Still staring at her, he murmured, 'If you insist your grandfather wasn't responsible, then why the letters? Not to claim kinship, obviously.'

'Kinship?' Her lovely face reflecting her complete and utter bewilderment, she queried slowly, 'Why on earth would I want to claim kinship?'

'To force acknowledgement, to let Phena know you were her niece.'

'Her niece?' she exclaimed incredulously. 'How could I be her niece?' When he opened his mouth, presumably to tell her, and confuse her further, she halted him with a shushing gesture. 'Let me get this straight. You thought my grandfather used your mother, then, when he found out she was pregnant, callously discarded her... And then you thought that when I found out— which I didn't, I hasten to add—I came to blackmail you, for money—or acceptance. Is that right? Is that what you're saying? Although why you should imagine I would want acceptance into your family when I have a perfectly good family of my own, I have no idea. Did your mother say Gramps was Phena's father? Well, did she?' she insisted. 'What's the matter, Feargal?' she taunted angrily when he remained silent. 'Afraid another little money-grubber might come knocking at your door claiming kinship? Or afraid that your mother might have lied?'

Continuing to stare at her, his face still hard, but with the added bonus of speculation, he said quietly, 'No.'

'No what? No she didn't lie? Or no, she didn't say he was the father?' Had Mrs McMahon known Gramps was incapable of fathering children? Obviously not, if that was the lie she was putting about. But why latch on to him as the father of her child? Because it was convenient? Expedient? Had Gramps even known that was the story she was telling? If indeed she had and it wasn't just Feargal's own assumptions. Watching him, she asked curiously, 'Did your father know? About Phena?'

'What? Yes, of course. He brought her up,' he said dismissively. 'She was two when he married my mother.'

'I see. It couldn't have been easy for her, a young unmarried mother, coming back to Ireland. Forty years ago they were a bit...'

'Judgemental? Yes, they were—but then, she didn't tell anyone, did she? She bought herself a ring and pretended she was a widow.'

'Did people believe her?'

'How the hell should I know? But it gave her a patina of respectability, and, as far as I know, only my father knew the truth, because she told him. And none of which—'

'And Phena? Does she know?' she interrupted.

'Oh, yes,' he agreed with a bitter little smile. 'She knows. She made it her business to find out. Another cross for us all to bear.'

'And you didn't want her to know about the letters because it would rake it all up again?'

'Yes.'

Feeling a twinge of guilt because she'd inadvertently brought it all up when all they wanted was for it to remain buried, and pushing aside for the moment the whys and wherefores of her grandfather's involvement, Ellie apologised quietly, 'I'm sorry. And of course I won't say anything. To anybody.'

'You're damned right you won't!' Staring at her, as though trying to make up his mind, he asked in that same flat, hard tone, 'Not blackmail?'

'No, of course not blackmail!'

'Not a family's revenge?'

'My family, do you mean? No! Why would they want revenge? It has nothing to do with them. Or me. I only brought the letters because Gramps asked me to...'

'And didn't it even once cross your mind that you might be doing harm?'

'No, how could it?' she justified. 'I didn't know there was a baby! Didn't know you thought...I mean, as far as I was aware, it was just an innocent friendship.'

'Friendship?' he demanded scathingly. 'Friendship? Even you can't be that naïve! He was old enough to be her father! A married man with two children! And you think that's all right? For a married man to be "friendly",' he mocked, 'seduce a seventeen-year-old girl, innocent and trusting, fresh over from Ireland? Or did that make her fair game?'

'No! And he didn't!' she denied forcefully.

'They found the baby under a bush?'

'Oh, don't be so ridiculous! And you never did answer me! Did your mother categorically state that Gramps was the father?'

'Yes!'

Yes? Oh, God, now what? Prove his mother a liar? Tell him it was an impossibility? Cause more trouble?

What would Gramps have done? Gone along with it? Perhaps he *had* gone along with it, and if he had, for whatever reason, agreed to the fiction, was it her place to undo it? Slumping back against the wall, she said wearily, 'Oh, I don't know! How could I, if Gramps didn't tell me?'

'Then I will tell you! He used her, discarded her, then paid her off and sent her back to Ireland! That's what happened! No romantic interlude! No overwhelming love-affair! Seduction, plain and simple!'

'No,' she denied. 'Oh, Feargal, no. Gramps wasn't like that.'

'You think he loved her?' he derided in disgust. 'Then decided he wasn't good enough for her? Played the proud hero and sent her home with enough money in her pocket to make a new start?'

'I don't know!' she insisted.

'Yes, Ellie, you do know,' he said quietly, in direct contrast to her stormy denial, 'and I can either believe that the letters were used merely as a passport for something else, or you are indeed a calculating little bitch intent only on causing pain.'

'Oh, for God's sake! Why would I want to cause anyone pain? Especially people I don't even know!'

'Because it would be a way to make money. And you certainly need money, don't you, Ellie?'

'No, I...'

'No?'

'No!' she gritted.

'And you without a job? Trying to manage on your giro? Dressing from charity shops...'

'That's by choice!' she snapped.

'Choice?' Glancing disparagingly down at the mismatched clothing, his mouth twisted. 'Do you really take me for a fool?'

'Yes,' she agreed, 'I'm beginning to think I do! You come out with these half-baked ideas; first I'm pursuing you, then I've come to blackmail your mother...'

'But it's all the same thing, isn't it, Ellie? So when was it you decided you'd like the money back?' he asked with the air of one who was prepared to enter into a lengthy discussion on the subject.

'What money back?'

'The conscience money he paid her.'

'I didn't know he'd paid her conscience money! And even if I had, and wanted it, I'd hardly keep insisting it wasn't him, would I?' she exclaimed. And it wasn't him! And if it wasn't, then who the hell had it been? With a little frown, she asked, 'How do you know he paid her?'

'How do you think?'

'Your mother told you?'

'No, I came across the letter that had been enclosed with the money when I was going through my father's papers after he died. Proof positive. Guilty money? Or for services rendered?'

'Don't,' she pleaded. 'Please don't; that makes your mother sound...'

'Like a tramp?'

'Yes, and you don't believe that, do you?'

'No, I don't believe that.'

No, because he believed her grandfather was a seducer. Not that she believed his mother was a tramp, but whatever had happened all those years ago it had obviously involved her grandfather—why else would he give her money when the child so obviously couldn't have been his? Obvious to her, at any rate. But if Gramps had known all this, why in heaven's name hadn't he warned her? Because he obviously didn't know of the fiction being put about. Perhaps he'd met her when she was pregnant, and had fallen in love with her? And because he couldn't marry her, but wanted her to be comfortable financially, had given her money? 'Perhaps they were in love,' she offered lamely.

'Love? Oh, come on! That's the stuff of fairy-tales!'

'It isn't!' she insisted. 'And perhaps he did think she would be better off without him!' Well, she would have had to be better off without him, wouldn't she? He was married! But until she could find out the truth from Mrs McMahon she'd have to tread warily, which meant continuing this absurd fiction. 'Haven't you ever loved anybody like that? Loved her more than life itself? Wanted to spare her pain?' And, needing desperately to defend her grandfather, she added weakly, 'Knowing he was too old for her, knowing that when the child grew up it would need a younger father...'

'He did the decent thing?' he derided.

'Yes! If he loved her enough. Well, haven't you ever loved like that?' she demanded desperately.

'No,' he denied flatly.

'Oh. Well, it could have happened that way. It's another explanation, isn't it? And people do behave like that...'

'Do they? Would you?' he asked nastily.

'I don't know,' she evaded, 'but that doesn't mean people don't!'

With scathing disregard for her feelings, he taunted, 'So he told her to take her baby and go? Return to her family in Ireland? Forget him?'

'Something like that, I suppose. I only saw the letters your mother wrote him, not the ones he wrote her.'

'So you did read them!'

'No! Just glanced at them to make sure there was nothing—well, nothing that might cause offence, or trouble,' she finished lamely.

'Trouble?' he scoffed. 'You don't call this trouble?'

Giving him a mutinous look, she defended for what felt the fortieth time, 'I didn't know about the baby!'

'And that makes it all right?' he asked incredulously.

'No, of course not. But how could I know? It wasn't done maliciously, with deliberate intent to wound!'

'Wasn't it? And yet you don't seem totally disappointed at the reaction you got! Or that the whole bloody circus will now start all over again.'

'Oh, Feargal!' she exclaimed weakly. 'I would dearly love to know why you keep sticking me with motives that I just don't have! And if Donal hadn't played such a stupid joke...'

'Donal? He knows about this?' he demanded angrily.

'No! But he knew I was coming to Slane, and, I suppose, because he knew you, knew you came from Slane, he thought it would be amusing to force us to meet...'

'For amusement?' he asked incredulously.

'Well, I know it sounds a bit odd, but what other reason could he have had?' With a little frown, she tried to think of another reason. Any reason... And did. Oh, God. Staring back at Feargal, she began hesitantly, 'I truly didn't know where your mother lived, except that it was Slane. Didn't know you, anything about you, and the only thing I can think of to explain it is that Maura, Donal's sister, told him the name of the family I was looking for. He knew you, your name, knew you came from Slane...'

'And so thought it would be amusing for us to meet before you came up here? *Amusing?*' he asked scathingly.

'Or helpful... Truly, Feargal, none of this was planned! I wish you'd believe me!'

'Yes, I just bet you do!'

'But it's true!' she insisted. 'Why are you being so blinkered? And Phena need never find out. Why should she? In which case there's no real harm been done, has there? *Has* there?' she persisted softly. 'And if your mother doesn't tell her...'

'Which still leaves us with why he sent them,' he said equally softly.

Oh, good grief. Wishing desperately that she were able to defend her grandfather, but knowing that to explain would only cause more trouble until she'd been able to speak with his mother, and fervently wishing she had locked her door when she'd come up to bed, Ellie said tiredly, 'I don't know why. Nor ever will now. He was old, Feargal, maybe confused; maybe he didn't even remember what they were about... I don't know. But is that why you don't like Phena?' she asked curiously. 'Because of what happened? Because she's only your half-sister?'

'No, and I don't dislike her, only the chip she has riding on her shoulder.'

'But *why* is she so bitter? Your father accepted her, didn't he?'

'Of course he accepted her! He loved her, loved my mother!'

'Then why?'

'Because she found out my mother lied to her! Because she was illegitimate! Because she spent endless time and money searching for her father, for the man on her birth certificate who didn't exist! For her mother's young husband who died!'

'Your mother didn't put my grandfather on the birth certificate?'

'No.'

'Oh.'

'Yes, oh! And because she can't accept that she isn't lady of the bloody manor after all!'

'Oh,' she repeated lamely.

With a tired shrug, he wandered over to the window and stared out at the grounds. 'She was the eldest,' he murmured in what sounded like reluctant explanation, 'but the farm and the house were left to me, as the eldest son. My father knew, as do I—who better?—' he retorted bitterly '—that she would have sold it, used the money for her own ends. She was adequately provided for—only it wasn't enough, and because she was angry, felt slighted perhaps, she went off to England to find her real family—Kent!' he added disgustedly.

'Kent?' Ellie asked in confusion. Where on earth had Kent come from?

'The name my mother put on the birth certificate as the child's father,' he explained impatiently as he turned to face her. 'David Anthony Kent. It was apparently the name they were going to use when he left his wife.'

'When he left his...? Who said he was going to leave his wife?' she demanded.

'He did!'

Oh, I don't believe any of this, she thought tiredly; every time she opened her mouth she got deeper and deeper into the mire. And of course Gramps had never left his wife—because he had never been going to, because he hadn't been the father; but that was obviously the story Marie O'Donnell had put about—the story her family believed. And then a nasty little thought popped into her brain. Not only had David Anthony been her grandfather's name, but the name he had given his adopted son. Oh, God. Was that it? Staring rather blankly at Feargal, she blinked and dragged her attention back to what he was saying.

'Only he didn't leave his wife, so Marie O'Donnell returned to Ireland, and because she knew how it would be if it was known she had an illegitimate child she told everyone she was a widow. That her young husband had died abroad—to explain the lack of a death certificate,' he tacked on. 'Neither did she admit to knowing where he was buried. So very convenient—and so very distressing for Phena.'

Knowing exactly what was coming next, and her heart aching for poor Phena, Ellie said softly, 'And she couldn't find any record of a David Anthony Kent having been born, having even existed—and so knew that her mother had lied.'

'Yes, and, determined to find out the truth, because Phena is nothing if not determined, she went to where my mother used to live.'

'How did she know where it was?' Ellie asked, puzzled. 'Surely your mother didn't tell her...'

'No, Mother's parents told her, not knowing of course why Phena wanted to know. They still had the letters the young Marie had written from England.'

'And?'

'By ill luck found someone who had known her.'

'And who unkindly told her the truth?'

'Yes. That she'd had no husband, that the only man she'd ever seen her with was—David Harland. The man my mother worked for. Just another little Irish girl who'd got herself into trouble.'

'Poor Phena.'

'Yes,' he agreed. 'Poor Phena.'

'Did she go and see my grandfather?'

'I don't know. She never said—surprisingly. She had plenty to say about everything else.'

'And now she's bitter?'

'Oh, yes. Now, she is very, very bitter. She has a house in Dublin,' he added inconsequentially.

Which you pay for? she wondered. 'I'm sorry,' she whispered again. And yet the woman she had met earlier didn't look bitter. She looked altogether charming.

'Oh, Mother denied it, of course, insisted he wasn't the father.'

'But later admitted it?' she asked fatalistically.

'Yes.'

'I see. Well, so long as no one tells Phena, everything should be all right, shouldn't it?' she asked with more hope than expectation.

'You'd better pray it is,' he warned.

'Well, Phena won't hear it from me! Anyway, I shan't be here, shall I? I'm to leave in the morning, remember?'

'And that really rankles, doesn't it? That's really what it's all about, isn't it? Wanting to stay here. Share in some of the wealth!'

'No, it is not! I don't need, or want, your blasted wealth!'

'Don't you? Then, just out of curiosity, who paid for the hotel in Dublin? It's one of the most expensive in the city. Got another poor sap on a string?'

'Another?' she asked sarcastically. 'That implies you think of yourself as a poor sap—and that, Feargal McMahon, you will never get me to believe! And, even though it's none of your business, for your information, my father paid for it.'

'Your father? I thought he was supposed to be making you stand on your own two feet? That's what you told me, isn't it?'

'Yes, but perhaps he thought I might meet some wealthy man who would instantly fall in love with me and so relieve him of some of the responsibility,' she retorted, too angry to even think what she was saying, and then gave a derisive smile when she saw that he was half tempted to believe it. 'Boy, wouldn't I dearly love to know why you have such a suspicious nature!'

'I'm sure you would. And if I hear so much as a whisper that you have been broadcasting our private affairs around the country...'

'You'll what? Beat me up?'

'Oh, no; I never use brute force when subtlety can be so much more effective.'

'You really think I'd do that?' she asked in hurt surprise.

'Yes, I do!' With a last withering glance, he walked across to the door and swung it wide, then gave a snort of disgust. Phena was outside.

'Not arguing again, Feargal,' she taunted sweetly. 'Or have I interrupted a little romantic interlude?'

'No,' he denied coldly, and with a last warning glance at Ellie he walked out.

'No romance?' she asked in mock disappointment.

'Sorry, no,' Ellie said dismissively, and if Phena thought she was also coming in for a chat she was mistaken. One member of the family had been quite enough. Although she hoped to God Phena hadn't heard anything she shouldn't. She didn't look as though she had, and surely if Feargal had thought so he wouldn't have left so abruptly? Too tired to even think about it now, she said firmly, 'Goodnight, Phena, I'll see you tomorrow, I expect. Before I leave.'

'You're leaving?' she asked in surprise.

'Yes.'

'Oh.' Giving Ellie a thoughtful look, she suddenly waggled her scarlet-tipped fingers, and walked away. To interrogate her brother?

Thankfully closing the door, Ellie trailed back to the bed. Nice opinion Feargal had of her, didn't he? And had she really expected anything else? And if she hadn't come? Then she would have saved herself a lot of grief. Perching on the side of the bed, she picked up Gwen Bear. 'I did all the wrong things for the best of reasons,' she whispered sadly. 'Does that make it right, or wrong? And is that what Gramps did, too? Because his adopted son was the father of Marie O'Donnell's baby? And he wouldn't, or didn't want to marry her?' It was pure speculation on her part—and yet there had been a family scandal, years ago, before her mother had married; she could vaguely remember her mother talking about it—and it had concerned her brother, Ellie's uncle. Perhaps she could ask when she got home. Although her mother wasn't the sort of person to tell you anything if it was something she didn't think you needed to know.

With a long sigh, and a great many troubled thoughts, Ellie got ready for bed. And in the morning she would have to have a very long talk with Feargal's mother. And then leave.

SHE WOKE WITH A START the next morning, confused and disorientated. Hearing Terry's voice out on the landing, she frowned, and climbed slowly from the bed. Opening her bedroom door, she peeped out. Terry was standing at the landing window, Rose just retreating down the stairs. Not sure of the reception she would get if she spoke to the other girl, not sure what her mother or Feargal might have told her, she was about to duck back into her room when Terry turned.

'Will you look at that?' she exclaimed, turning back to point at the grounds.

Moving along the landing to join her, Ellie too peered out, and to her astonishment saw a crowd of Japanese tourists, cameras at the ready, wandering down the path.

'Where the devil did they come from at this time in the morning? It's only eight o'clock, for God's sake!'

'I don't know,' Ellie said stupidly, and Terry burst out laughing.

'No, I don't suppose you do. Unless you're trying to swell the family coffers all by yourself. Are you all right?' she asked gently. 'I heard about the ruckus.'

'Yes, so, sadly, I won't after all be here for the wedding . . .'

'You won't?' Terry exclaimed. 'But why?'

'Because I've been given my marching orders,' Ellie said more shortly than she'd intended. 'Because he won't believe that I'm not a cheat and a liar . . .'

'Oh, he'll get over that,' Terry said with the confidence of a sister who didn't know her brother as well as she thought she did. 'He likes you, I can tell.' Then, with a rather dubious air, she murmured, 'Well, I think I can. The trouble is, he's a bit of a cynic. Mind,' she added fairly, 'I suppose he has some justification; even

I have to admit that he's the most devastating-looking man this side of the Boyne, and women do tend to try and—er—interest him.'

'But I wasn't trying to interest him!' Ellie denied in horror.

'Weren't you?' she teased. When Ellie went scarlet, because there was definitely more than a grain of truth in that statement, she laughed, not unkindly. 'Never mind, Ellie, but you must understand that what with one thing and another we do tend to jump to conclusions—not always the most obvious.'

They did? Why? Because that was the way things were? Or because they had specific reasons?

'And aren't I the one forever telling people to find out the facts first? I should practise what I preach is what I should do,' Terry continued.

'That still doesn't alter the fact that I have to leave,' Ellie pointed out quietly.

'No, you don't. I know Feargal lammed into you,' she added wryly, 'but he doesn't mean the half of what he says when he's in a temper. But—oh, Ellie, there was such a to-do last time, Phena carrying on as though she were the only person in the world who had been lied to, and I know it was hard for her, and Feargal would have given her all this without a blink, but she wanted to play the martyr, and now makes him pay for it in oh, so many little ways.'

'But why blame Feargal?'

'Because he inherited, and because she knows he feels guilty, and so plays on it. The truth is, Ellie, Phena is not a very *nice* person. I know that's a wicked thing to say about my half-sister, but she isn't. Wasn't even before all this came out. She's the most awful snob. And now she's bitter as well. Poor old Feargal,' she sighed softly. 'We all, in our various ways, dump our troubles on him, expect him to sort them out. Even Mother, and though I love her dearly she doesn't seem to realise that he doesn't have the time to run after her the way Dad used to. She took to the good life like a duck to water,' she added wryly.

'She didn't come from a wealthy family?'

'Lord, no. They weren't desperate or anything, but nothing like Dad, and he only had the farm to run. Feargal has a lot of other interests as well, and first and foremost he's a businessman—needs to be, to keep us lot! But Mum's used to having things done for her, you see. Father spoiled her rotten. I dump on him too,' she added guiltily. 'And the sad thing is, it's a habit very hard to break because he's always so damned competent—and we all in our various ways expect his uncomplaining support. Expect him to pay for all our needs, solve all our little problems—'

Breaking off, she gave a little snort of laughter. 'You have to admire him, though, don't you? Look at him, lord of all he surveys, calm, controlled, in total command of himself. Anyone else would be tearing his hair out, confronted by a pack of jabbering foreigners, but does Feargal? No, he calmly surveys them, holds his hands up for silence—and I know for a fact he can't speak a word of Japanese.'

Peering past Terry's shoulder, Ellie stared down at Feargal, the dog at his heels, confronting a crowd of people all waving their arms about—and Terry was right, he didn't look in the least fazed. Arrogant—but not daunted. And she didn't want to be at odds with him, didn't want him to think her a cheat—only what were the odds on him ever believing otherwise? Not very good, if not impossible. And then Ellie was exasperated with herself for even caring. He'd been damned rude to her the night before, not to say insulting.

'I'd best go down and see if I can help, I suppose.'

'Can you speak Japanese?' Ellie asked in mock admiration.

'No,' Terry laughed. 'Can you?' When Ellie shook her head, she said, 'I'll see you later—and don't leave!' she warned. 'Or at least, if you insist on doing so, don't go before I come back!' With a backward wave, she hurried down the stairs.

Returning to her room, Ellie washed and dressed, and rather dispiritedly began to pack. Kneeling on the floor, trying to force her case closed, she heard Terry calling her, and the sound of footsteps hurrying up the stairs.

'Ellie?' Terry called as she burst into the room. 'Ellie, can you cook?' she demanded urgently.

'A bit. Why?'

'Because those wretched Japanese are all demanding breakfast and we don't normally open the restaurant until ten-thirty for morning coffee so there's no one there to cook it! Rose and Mary don't come in till midday and it's more than my life's worth to go and ask them to come in early, and Feargal is in desperate need of some help!'

'What about Phena?'

'Phena?' she asked in astonishment. 'Phena wouldn't know a soup ladle from a hoe! And even if she did she'd never get her hands dirty helping in a *kitchen!*'

'Oh, right,' Ellie agreed somewhat blankly.

'And I have to go to work!'

'Oh.'

'Well, don't just be kneeling there, Ellie Browne with an "E"! Move!' she grinned.

'Right.' Scrambling to her feet, Ellie ran after the racing Terry, down the stairs, out the back door, across the grounds and in through the back door of the restaurant. Although why she was hurrying to help Feargal, she had no idea. He certainly didn't deserve any! Not from her, at any rate.

Looking up, he gave his sister a faint smile. Ellie he ignored. 'They don't speak English,' he informed her, 'and despite my attempts to persuade them differently they just all trooped in and sat down. The kettle's on; it will have to be instant coffee—there's no time to percolate any.' Still totally ignoring Ellie, he continued, 'I'll go and get some eggs and bread.' And then he was gone.

'Lord, Ellie, but I'm going to be fearful late for school!' Terry exclaimed as she hastily opened cupboards and showed Ellie where everything was.

'School?' she asked foolishly.

'Yes! I'm the teacher!' Glancing at her watch, she groaned. 'I have to go!'

And she did, leaving a very bewildered Ellie to look round her at the well-equipped kitchen and the gently steaming kettle. Spotting a hatch in the far wall, she walked across and gingerly opened it a crack. Oh, good grief! There were hundreds of them! All sitting, chattering away like starlings. Taking a deep, calming breath, she closed the hatch, arranged the row of sugar bowls on a tray and determinedly walked out into the restaurant. The sudden silence was terrifying. Pinning a bright smile on her face, she carefully placed a sugar bowl on each table, beamed at them all impartially, scurried back for the pile of menus on the counter— only to have them forcibly removed from her hands by Feargal.

'They're lunch menus.' Reaching under the counter, he handed her a pile of printed sheets. 'Give those out and pray that even if they can't speak English they can at least read it!'

'Please,' she prompted.

The look he gave her decided her not to press him. Her forced smile still in place, she handed out the sheets, then went back to the kitchen and grabbed the pad and pencil that was thrust at her.

'Where's Terry?' he demanded as he expertly spooned instant coffee into numerous cups.

'Gone to school. She was late!'

She didn't quite catch what he muttered under his breath, and, deciding it would be exceedingly foolish to ask him to repeat it, fled back to the restaurant.

Everyone beamed at her. Oh, heavens. In slow, careful English, she asked the gentlemen at the first table, 'You are ready to order?'

A fountain of incomprehensible Japanese flooded over her. I see, she thought. Fine. She felt an overwhelming desire to giggle. Taking the menu out of the nearest gentleman's hand, she laid it flat on the table, and with her pencil pointed to the first item, then mimed drinking. Beside the line offering coffee, she drew a little cup and saucer. A little clap greeted this brilliant improvisation. He jabbered away to his friends, and Ellie assumed he was explaining that item number one was a drink. Encouraged by this, she drew pictures all the way down the menu, and with a great deal of giggling all round she returned triumphantly to the kitchen.

'Sixteen coffees,' she announced in the cool voice that they seemed to be using to each other, 'followed by—

er—' Consulting her list, she continued, 'Six rounds of toast, five boiled eggs with soldiers . . .'

'With what?' he asked incredulously.

'Soldiers. Two eg—'

'We don't do soldiers . . .'

'Yes, we do,' she interrupted. 'We just cut the buttered bread into strips. Two eggs on toast . . .'

'Poached or fried?' he asked sarcastically.

'Fried,' she informed him nicely. 'They didn't seem to understand my drawing of poaching—and three bowls of rice crispies.'

'We don't do rice crispies.'

'Feargal!' she exclaimed in exasperation. 'We do rice crispies! They might look like cornflakes,' she added in inspiration as she saw the packet on the shelf, 'but, believe me, they're rice crispies!'

'May the saints preserve us,' he muttered. 'OK. Put the toast in while I take out their coffees, then put the big frying-pan on.' Giving her a bland look, obviously forgetting to be cold, he asked sarcastically, 'How long do they want their eggs boiled for?'

'Three minutes,' she said with a perfectly straight face.

He took out the coffees.

Half an hour later, they sat nursing their own coffees amid the debris in the kitchen, the warmth of which wasn't quite enough to effect a thaw between them.

'I still don't think you should have charged them,' Ellie repeated, for at least the third time.

'Of course I should have charged them! It's not a philanthropic society!'

'I know it isn't, but—well, it wasn't very professionally done,' she added worriedly. 'The eggs looked a bit . . .'

'Fried!' he put in determinedly. 'You can't expect fried eggs to be all tidy. And they didn't complain!'

'How would you know? You can't speak Japanese!'

'They looked happy!' he declared with an air that said the subject was now closed. As he glanced down at the menu in his hand, the one with the pictures down the side, she could have sworn he was trying very hard not to smile.

'You could have them printed like that,' she said slyly.

'Mm.'

'Well, it worked, didn't it?'

'Yes, Ellie,' he agreed. 'It worked.' Glancing round him at the mess, he added coolly, 'We'd best clear up before Mary arrives. She'll have a fit otherwise.'

Much to her surprise, he helped her. She had sort of expected him to leave it all to herself. He might be lord of all he surveyed, but it seemed he didn't in the least mind getting his own hands dirty, even it if was to assist his arch enemy.

When the kitchen had been restored to its former tidiness, he gave her a curt nod, and walked out. Thank you, Ellie, it was so kind of you to help. Oh, that's all right. Pulling a little face, she carefully folded the tea-towel she'd been using and laid it on the work surface. And if she hadn't brought those stupid letters, if they hadn't had a row about them, it could have been fun working with him. Could, Ellie, could. Episode over, put it out of your mind. Go and find his mother, get an explanation, and then leave.

Unfortunately, Mrs McMahon was nowhere to be found. Avoiding her? Well, she wasn't leaving until she'd sorted this muddle out. Feeling hungry, Ellie made herself some toast in the kitchen, collected some brochures from the hall table, and took herself out for the day. She would find Mrs McMahon when she came back, and Feargal could make of that what he would.

CHAPTER FIVE

WHEN SHE RETURNED to the house in late afternoon, Ellie's determination to put a few pertinent questions to Mrs McMahon and then leave was thwarted—deliberately, probably—by Feargal, who was with his mother in the lounge.

'Still here, Ellie?' he asked in mock surprise.

Halting on the threshold in frustration, she gave him a sweet smile. 'Yes; I wanted to have a word with your mother.'

'Hello, Ellie,' Mrs McMahon greeted, waving her forward, yet her smile seemed false—and rather desperate. Had Feargal been asking her questions she had no wish to answer? Much like the questions Ellie herself wanted the answers to?

'Feargal has just been telling me how you helped out this morning, and your idea of putting pictures on the menus. That was kind of you—and clever.'

Surprised that he had even told anyone, let alone complimented her in her absence, Ellie looked at him in astonishment—which was a waste of time, because he had found something quite riveting to stare at in the fireplace.

'And did you have a good day?' his mother persisted.

'Yes. I went to Newgrange.'

'And what did you think?'

Giving in to the inevitable, and until she had found out the truth she had as yet no quarrel with his mother, Ellie relaxed her rigid stance. It was very difficult to remain frosty in the face of someone's desperate attempts to be friendly. 'It was awfully clean,' she stated impressively. 'As though someone had just scrubbed the place out. Not a speck of dust to be found!' With her enchanting grin, which had, sadly, not been much in evidence of late, she added, 'I expect Sheila from down the road had been in with her "Mr Sheen"...' With a comical grimace in the face of their blank incomprehension, she substituted, 'It didn't seem old. I mean not Bronze Age, or whatever, and a calf was eating the grass on the top as though—well, as though it didn't matter.'

'You think we just built it for the tourists?' Feargal asked silkily.

Ignoring him, Ellie continued to smile at Mrs McMahon.

'And where else did you go?' the older woman asked quickly.

'Oh, to Navan, and then to Trim, and then I came back. And I saw a dear little shed that someone had made into a craft shop, and the woman said no one had been in for ages, and wasn't she pleased to see me...'

'So you felt you had to buy something?'

'Mm. A woolly hat. It will be warm for the winter...' Withdrawing one hand from behind her back, she held it up for inspection. 'She didn't have any bags to put it in.'

'And did you go to see Mellifont Abbey?'

'No—perhaps I'll call in as I leave,' she added pointedly for Feargal's benefit.

'You'll not stay for the wedding? No,' Mrs McMahon answered herself sadly with a quick glance at her son, 'perhaps it's best not.' Yet she'd sounded genuinely disappointed that Ellie wouldn't be there. She shouldn't have been—should have been glad to be rid of her.

'Mm,' Ellie agreed lamely, 'but I would like to speak to you before I go. Alone.' Mrs McMahon looked flustered, and Feargal turned his head to stare at her. 'And perhaps you'll tell me how much I owe for my board and lodging,' she added.

'I don't think,' he said in a quiet, deadly voice, 'that you will ever be able to pay what you owe.'

Holding his gaze for a moment, she sighed. 'Perhaps not, but it was an inadvertent debt, Feargal; I wish you'd believe that.'

'Yes, I dare say you do.' With a curt nod, he straightened, and walked out. The door was closed very carefully behind him. And would he now stand outside and listen? Probably. Or had the room been wired for sound? Switching her gaze to his mother, Ellie said quietly, 'We have to talk.'

'No, I . . .'

'Yes,' Ellie insisted gently, but firmly. 'And although it's not strictly my business, and I don't want to pry into things that aren't my concern, I do need to know why you told everyone that Gramps was Phena's father— No . . .' With a little shake of her head, she changed it to, 'I need to know if Gramps knew that's what you'd said.'

'How do you know he wasn't the father?' Mrs McMahon asked quietly.

'Because he couldn't have children,' Ellie stated simply. 'His son and daughter were adopted.'

Staring at Ellie in astonishment, the older woman suddenly began to laugh quietly. 'Oh, my! Trust me to choose the one man that would make it impossible. And trust him not to ever say.'

'So he did know?'

'Yes, Ellie, of course he knew. I'm not entirely without principles,' she reproved.

'No, sorry, I didn't mean to imply...'

'I know.' Leaning back in her chair, Mrs McMahon gave a long sigh. 'I think I always knew that it would come out one day. Skeletons have a habit of breaking out of closets, don't they? And usually at the most inopportune moment. Sit down, child, this is not going to be—easy.'

Doing as she was told, Ellie asked hesitantly, 'Was it his son who...?'

'His son? Good heavens, no! Whatever gave you that idea?'

'The name on the birth certificate, I suppose. Feargal said it was David Anthony Kent. Both Gramps and his son had the name David Anthony, and if it wasn't Gramps...'

'I see. Feargal seems to have said a great deal. And why not if he thinks you know it all already? I'm sorry, Ellie; I let you in for a hard time, didn't I?'

With a wry smile, Ellie admitted, 'It wouldn't have been so hard if I'd known what he was talking about.'

'No,' she sighed. Then, holding the younger woman's eyes for a moment, she asked, 'Can I trust you, Ellie?'

'Yes, of course.'

'And if anyone's owed an explanation it's you.' Keeping her voice low, Mrs McMahon began, 'I'll not tell you his name—I'll not tell anyone his name; that will go to the grave with me—but he wasn't English, Ellie. I was pregnant before I ever left Ireland.'

'Before?'

'Yes, not that I knew it at the time, of course, else I'd never have gone.' Her gaze distant, as though she was looking back into the past, she continued, 'It wouldn't have been easy, staying here, but I dare say we would have managed. My family weren't wealthy, couldn't have afforded to send me away till it was over, couldn't have kept it secret, so perhaps it's just as well it turned out as it did. I told you about your grandfather giving me a job, didn't I? And everything would have been fine, except of course nature took its course and I could no longer pretend that I wasn't pregnant. He found me one day, crying my heart out, and because he was the sort of man he was—kind, sympathetic—I told him. It was he who arranged medical care, arranged the hospital—even arranged for an adoption; but once I'd had the baby, and she so soft and little, so lovely, I couldn't do it. And him being a lawyer and all, we cooked up a grand scheme between us so that I could go back to Ireland with my pride intact.'

'And everyone thought it was Gramps who was the father?'

'Not then, no, because the scheme we'd concocted was that my "husband" was a soldier, who'd died abroad, and everyone would, hopefully, have continued to believe it, if Phena hadn't flounced off to England to discover her roots! And how can I blame her for that? Instead, she discovered your grandfather, and put two and two together and made five. And, to my shame, I thought how much easier it would be to let them all believe it. I wrote to him, asked what I should do, and he said let it lie. And I truly don't think he minded.'

'No,' Ellie agreed. 'He would probably have smiled his gentle smile and said, "Do what you think is best." Did Phena go to see him?'

'I don't know. She wouldn't say, and neither would David.'

'And the real father? Could he not have married you?'

'No, he was already married, you see, a marriage he could never escape from, no matter how much he might have wanted to. He never even knew the baby was his. It wouldn't have been fair.'

'You loved him?'

'Yes,' she said simply. 'I've always loved him, and that's a burden I alone must bear... I loved Tom McMahon too—you mustn't be thinking I didn't, that I cheated him, but it was a different sort of love. Not any the less for being that—just different.'

'I see.' And if her grandfather had agreed, who was she to say different? Best to let sleeping dogs lie. 'Is that what those letters were? You writing to ask what you should do?'

'Yes.'

'Then they should definitely be burned. I wonder why Gramps didn't? Or ask me to?'

'I don't know, and they are burned. I destroyed them last night. I only kept the little note that was with them, and the statuette, of course.'

'So there's no way Phena could find out—and I certainly shan't tell her!'

'Nor I!' Mrs McMahon exclaimed with a shudder. With a faint, sad smile, she asked, 'Does it hurt you, Ellie? For everyone to think he was a—seducer?'

'Hurt? No, not hurt exactly, sad, a bit angry that Feargal should think he was less than he was. He was good, and kind, and gentle, and I loved him very much. Got on better with him than my own parents,' she said wistfully.

'And still miss him?'

'Yes.'

'I'm sorry, Ellie, but can you bear just to bite your tongue when he sounds off about him? It's a lot to ask, I know, and my son can be very forceful sometimes.'

'Forceful?' Ellie queried with a wry smile. 'He was downright savage, as I recall!'

'Mm,' she agreed, 'we're all blessed with a bit of a temper, I'm afraid.'

Blessed? Was that what it was?

'And now, knowing the truth, or as much as I'm prepared to divulge, will you not stay for the wedding? Let me try and make up for my son's suspicions? Just a few more days? Please? I've enjoyed having you here, and in a small way it will sort of thank David, make it up to him by having his granddaughter to stay. He did so much for me, Ellie, won't you let me do just a small bit for you? You don't have much money, do you?'

'No,' she agreed with her funny little grimace.

'Then stay. Please? I'll make it right with Feargal.'

Will you? How? Ellie thought. 'I don't think that's really a very good idea. He was pretty emphatic about me leaving. But what I'd dearly love to know is what on earth made him so suspicious of me? He didn't even seem to consider for a moment that I might be innocent. Did something like this happen before?'

'Not to my knowledge, but you have to understand... Oh, heavens, I don't know how to say this without sounding conceited, but—well, he's something rather special, my son. Not only clever, but extraordinarily attractive to women—and wealthy, of course, and it's a sad fact of life that there are people in this world who only see money, only see advantage—and you wouldn't believe the number of begging letters he receives. The charities, the women—beautiful women, some of them, but so shallow, Ellie, so very shallow, and I think my son became disillusioned very early in life. My heart aches for him sometimes, but I'm blessed if I know if he's happy; if he ever wants to marry, have a family, he keeps his thoughts, feelings very much to himself. And I don't think that's always a good thing.' With another smile for the younger girl, she persisted, 'So will you? Just for a few more days?'

'I'd like to, but I really don't think I should. It's bound to cause friction, and that's not fair with Terry's wedding coming up. No, I really think it might be best if I go.'

'I suppose,' the older woman agreed reluctantly. 'Well, will you come and view my wedding outfit first? Give me your opinion?'

'Why?' Ellie teased. 'Aren't you sure about it?'

'No,' she said wryly. 'I have a horrible feeling it makes me look like a daffodil!'

Laughing, Ellie agreed. 'OK. One look at the outfit, and then I'll go.'

'Thank you.' Getting to her feet, Mrs McMahon gave Ellie a warm hug just as Feargal walked in. 'I'll go and get it out. Come on up when you're ready.' With a vague smile for her son, she walked out.

'What was all that about?' he asked coolly.

'Nothing—except that your mother asked me to have a look at her wedding outfit before I go. Did Phena say anything to you?' she asked. 'About overhearing anything I mean?'

'No, and I doubt very much that she did, otherwise I wouldn't have left it as I did. This is an old house, the walls are very thick, as are the doors.'

'Oh, so you were unable to hear what your mother and I were talking about?' she asked naughtily.

His blue eyes were steady, unwavering, and after a moment's silence he said softly, 'You do love to push your luck, don't you?'

'Mm. Makes life—interesting, wouldn't you say? And now, if you'll excuse me.'

'Certainly, but before you go I would be interested to learn whether Mother managed to convince you that your grandfather was to blame. If indeed you needed convincing.'

Looking down, finding it very difficult to lie, she nodded. 'Yes,' she agreed quietly. 'Your mother has explained.'

'Good. Poor Ellie,' he commiserated mockingly. 'How you must be wishing you'd chosen a different way of doing things.'

'Well, I'm certainly wishing I'd never heard of the wretched letters, that's for sure!' she exclaimed, recovering her spirit. 'Or caused trouble that was never meant.'

'And isn't that just the worst of it all?' he asked with a bitter smile. 'Trouble that's not meant to be caused?'

'Yes.' What else could she say?

Taking her completely by surprise, he caught hold of her arm and pulled her towards him. Staring down into her wide eyes, he concluded quietly, 'Although I think, Elinor Browne, that you would cause trouble by just being alive.'

'It would certainly seem so in this instance, wouldn't it?' she asked with some of his own bitterness, and then she was quite unable to tear her eyes away from his. So blue, so bright, they made her feel mesmerised and shaky, and, hating herself for standing meekly while she was being insulted, she hardened her expression. And yet the shaming thing was, she wanted him to hold her, kiss her as he had before. Wanted it very much. And wasn't that a joke by the gods? To actually meet a man she didn't find boring, a man who could make her feel, and to know that nothing could ever come of it?

'And isn't it a terrible thing to be bringing even more trouble down upon my head? Quite willingly,' he murmured against her mouth.

Hardly daring to breathe, hardly daring to even think, she closed her eyes in a sort of helpless defeat. One last kiss—and it was all that she wanted and more. Like coming home. Long and slow, powerful enough to tear the heart right out of her. It seemed to go on for a very long time. There was no arrogance in it, no anger, just a gentle exploration that deepened imperceptibly until hunger and passion hovered just on the periphery, deliberately held at bay.

'You feel warm and soft, and altogether too tempting, Ellie Browne,' he whispered. Moving her just a fraction away, his eyes once more holding hers captive, he added, 'So isn't it fortunate that I know you for the cheat you are?'

As though she had been doused in cold water, she stiffened and moved away. 'And isn't it fortunate that I know you for a blind fool?'

His smile was twisted, derisive. 'Even more than you know,' he admitted strangely. 'Go on, run away, Ellie. Go and view the outfit—and then leave. I shan't see you again—I'm leaving in a few moments to drive down to

Kildare. I have a horse running tomorrow at the Curragh.'

'The Curragh?' she asked blankly.

'Home of the Irish Derby. I shall be taking Phena with me.'

'How nice for you. And will it win? Your horse?'

'I hope so.'

'More money for your coffers? More money to offer your God?'

'Is that what you think?'

Turning away from him, she shook her head. 'No,' she denied wearily. 'Goodbye, Feargal.' Without looking at him again, she walked out. Feeling shaken and hurt, she walked quietly upstairs. Standing on the landing, she took a moment or two to compose herself, then walked the last few feet to his mother's room. The door was open, and she halted on the threshold and stared in astonishment at the collection of memorabilia that littered every available surface. Photographs, ornaments jammed anyhow on to whatever might accommodate them; furniture, chairs and tallboys that seemed to fight for space. Shaking her head in bemusement, she moved her gaze to the outfit spread out on the bed, and didn't quite have time to screw her face into an expression of approval before Mrs McMahon looked at her.

'No?'

'Well, it's very nice...'

'But not me?' she asked dubiously as she held it up against her.

'It takes all your colour,' she began hesitantly, 'and I know I hardly look as though I would know which colour went with what, or what suited whom...'

'You dress that way from choice, not because you have no idea how to?'

'Mm.' Feeling wretched and embarrassed, Ellie offered impulsively, 'I could run you into Dublin tomorrow and you could perhaps change it for something else. Feargal won't be here, so he needn't know that I haven't left yet.'

'Really?' Mrs McMahon asked in obvious surprise. 'You'd do that? After—well, after...'

'The misunderstandings?' Ellie offered helpfully. 'Yes, of course.'

'Because we can't have the bride's mother looking like a daffodil?' Staring at the outfit with a suddenly jaundiced eye, Feargal's mother muttered, 'I knew it was a mistake. Lord, Ellie, other people don't seem to have the trouble I do choosing an outfit. Why can't I ever find things that suit me?'

'Because you get fed up with looking,' she guessed with a smile. 'Because you can't be doing with it.'

'Yes,' she agreed, tossing the offending garment back on to the bed. 'I *hate* shopping! And so generally buy the first thing that actually fits. That's also why I didn't have it made!' she added comically. 'I mean, if I can't choose something that's actually there and I can try on, what chance would I have just looking at pictures?'

Laughing, Ellie said she didn't know.

'I wish you were staying for it!' she exclaimed sadly. 'You could, you know! Would you have anything to wear?'

'I don't know,' Ellie hedged without any clear idea whether she had or she hadn't. Certainly nothing smart or elegant, although there was that red velvet dress...
'I have a red velvet dress...' she began with one of her

delightful slow smiles. 'Only it might not quite be what you'd think acceptable.'

'If you think it's acceptable, and you feel comfortable in it, does it matter?'

'Well, yes, it does; I wouldn't want to...'

'Let us all down by looking like the poor relation?' Mrs McMahon teased. 'We'll say you're eccentric.'

'Could have said I was eccentric,' argued gently.

With a sigh, she gave in. 'All right, Ellie, I expect you know best. And will you really take me into Dublin tomorrow?'

'Yes, of course.'

'You're a good girl; I do wish things could have been different.' Eyeing the yellow creation tossed negligently on to the bed, the older woman burst out laughing. 'Perhaps I ought to wear the wretched thing after all, just to give a talking-point. Oh, well, come on; let's go down and see what's for dinner. I don't know about you, but I'm starving.'

CHAPTER SIX

As soon as she'd finished breakfast the following morning, Ellie went in search of Mrs McMahon. She felt oddly guilty at defying Feargal—not that he would know, but still. What a muddle life was. And disappointing.

'Ready?' she asked quietly when she ran her to earth in the lounge.

'Yes, of course. Now you're sure you don't mind? I can easily ask Feargal to take me tomorrow.'

'Oh, I'm sure Feargal would be delighted to run you into Dublin,' Ellie agreed with a teasing smile. 'No trouble at all.'

'Well, he would, if I insisted,' Mrs McMahon grinned, 'only I'm not fool enough to do so. Come along, then; let's try and change the dratted suit.'

Ellie had known that Mrs McMahon was not a forceful or decisive person, but hadn't quite realised just how easily led she was. And although they managed to change the yellow suit quite easily another disastrous creation would have been bought in its place had Ellie not been with her. All it took was for one saleslady to tell her she looked lovely and Mrs McMahon was persuaded. Ellie had to be very firm. And perhaps, the little thought persisted, Feargal would not view her quite so badly if she actually did something that couldn't be misinterpreted.

They eventually found something that she thought perfect. A dark pink, classically cut suit, with darker pink hat and gloves to match. 'Now that,' Ellie enthused, 'looks lovely!'

'It does, doesn't it?' she exclaimed in surprise. 'I didn't know I could look like that. Elegant and sort of—young! Thank you, Ellie, you're a kind girl.'

They drove back to Slane, completely in charity— Ellie pleased that she had been able to help, Mrs McMahon delighted that she wouldn't, after all, look a fright.

'If you'll kindly drop me off in the village, I have one or two things to do. I'll walk back to the Hall.'

'OK,' Ellie agreed quietly. 'I'd best say goodbye now, then, hadn't I?'

'Oh!' Mrs McMahon exclaimed, disconcerted. 'Oh, Ellie, I forgot all about you leaving!'

'That's all right. It was lovely to meet you, and perhaps if you ever come over to England . . .'

'Yes,' she agreed sadly, but she didn't look as though she thought it might be a possibility. 'Oh, drat Feargal and his suspicions! Although, to be fair, if Phena, for whatever reason, did find out that you were David's granddaughter we'd never hear the last of it.'

'Mm.' Bending forward, Ellie dropped a light kiss on the other woman's cheek. 'I hope everything goes well for the wedding. Bye,' she whispered.

With an unhappy sigh, Mrs McMahon got out at the crossroads, and, feeling choked, Ellie drove on to the hall to drop off the suit, and collect her own luggage.

Walking despondently upstairs, and into Mrs McMahon's bedroom to leave the outfit, she came to a shocked halt. Phena was in there, rifling through her mother's jewel case.

'No need to look so horrified,' Phena drawled, 'I wasn't stealing mother's jewels.'

'No, I didn't suppose you were; sorry, I just didn't expect to see you—I thought you were still out with Feargal.' Holding up the suit bag, Ellie explained, 'I just came to leave this.'

'We came back early,' she said with a shrug before going back to her rifling. Picking up a sheet of paper, she casually unfolded it, and then gave an exclamation. Turning to stare at Ellie, who was rather horrified by Phena's behaviour—something she would never have done to her own mother—she accused, 'You're his granddaughter!'

'What?' Ellie asked warily.

'David Harland! You're his granddaughter! And letters, it says!' Thrusting the paper under Ellie's, she demanded, 'What damned letters?'

'I don't know,' Ellie denied numbly as she recognised the note Gramps had put in with the package to Mrs McMahon.

'Don't lie! "Ellie has kindly offered to bring the letters back to you," it says. So what letters?'

'I don't know,' Ellie repeated stubbornly, 'and you shouldn't be reading private notes . . .'

'Shouldn't? Shouldn't?' she screeched. 'You think I don't have the right to know what's being said behind my back?'

'Nothing was said behind your back!' Then, gripping her lips firmly together, because whatever else she said was bound to be wrong, Ellie continued to stare at Phena in horror and worry.

With a little sneer, Phena retorted softly, 'Niece.'

'No.'

'No? You aren't his granddaughter?'

'Yes, but...'

'But what?' a cold voice asked from behind her.

Swinging round, she stared at Feargal, then slumped in defeat. 'I didn't, wasn't... Oh, hell!' she exclaimed wearily.

'Oh, hell indeed,' he said tonelessly.

'Well, well, well, another one in on the plot,' Phena said nastily. 'Hello, brother mine, what perfect timing you do have. Ellie was just about to explain about the letters.'

'No, I wasn't!' she denied forcefully.

Ignoring Ellie, he walked across to his sister and twitched the note out of her hand. Glancing down, he read it, then crumpled it. 'Singularly foolish of Mother to leave it lying around.'

'Yes, but then Mother is singularly foolish, isn't she?' Phena taunted bitterly. 'And are we now to welcome Ellie into the fold? Clothe her, feed her, give her an allowance? Or am I supposed to share mine with her?'

'No!' Ellie exclaimed.

'No,' Feargal denied as though Ellie hadn't spoken.

'So why is she here? And don't, please, tell me it was out of the goodness of her heart,' she derided, 'because that I won't believe.'

'I don't know why she came,' he asserted. 'Don't in fact know why she is still here,' he added pointedly.

'Because I ran your mother into Dublin to get a new wedding outfit. Came in here to leave it, and...'

'And discovered me rifling through mother's jewel box,' Phena finished.

'For what reason?' Feargal asked.

'Earrings, sweetness,' she retorted sarcastically. 'My earrings that I lent Mother last time I was here.'

'And found the note?'

'Yes, and wasn't it nice that little Ellie was here just in time to help clarify things?'

'There's nothing to clarify. There was nothing in the letters that you didn't already know,' Feargal said.

'Then why did she bring them?'

'Again, I do not know. Why not ask her yourself?'

Turning to the silent Ellie, Phena asked sweetly, 'Well?'

With a long sigh, Ellie said woodenly, 'Because Gramps asked me to.'

'And did he have any little messages for me? His long-lost daughter?'

'No.'

'No,' she echoed. 'Why should I expect anything else? Everyone but me,' she bit out viciously. 'And shouldn't I have been the first person to have known about them? But oh, no, let's keep them from Phena! Let's pretend they don't exist! No one, not one of you, had the courage to tell me!'

Walking across to his sister, Feargal put a gentle hand on her shoulder. 'There was nothing to tell,' he told her quietly.

'Nothing to tell?' she exclaimed in astonishment as she shrugged violently away from his touch. 'When here is proof positive that he's my father?' Grabbing Ellie's wrist in punishing fingers, she spat, 'Do you have any idea how it feels to be no one?'

'But you are someone,' Ellie protested.

'No! I don't *belong!* But you do, don't you, Ellie? Oh, yes, little Ellie Browne belongs—and now hopes to belong somewhere else. Like here!'

'No!'

'No? You don't covet my delightful, rich brother?' she sneered. 'Or is it only his lifestyle? Best be quick,

Ellie, he's much sought after. He has a great deal of land, his fingers in numerous profit-making pies, owns racehorses—and, of course, the added bonus of being extremely attractive to women. And, although I'm not so bitchy as to suggest women want him only for what they can get, nine times out of ten it's probably the truth.'

Her face reflecting her disgust, and horror as she stared at the other woman, Ellie turned to glance at Feargal to see how he might be taking this insulting piece of arrant mischief-making, and was astonished to see that he looked not angry, but almost sad. Because the poison inside his sister hurt him more than her accusations?

'I don't covet anything that any of you have,' Ellie said simply. 'And I find it rather sad that both of you should think I do—be so suspicious of everyone's motives. It must made life very—complicated.'

'Complicated? Oh, complicated, I'll grant you. It's always been bloody complicated! And totally unfair!'

'Only because you've allowed it to be. And you can't really believe that women only want your brother for his mon—'

'Be quiet,' Feargal commanded coldly. 'I don't need you to defend me.'

'I don't suppose you do. But you can't expect me to stand here meekly...'

'I don't expect anything but your silence. Go on, Phena.'

Her face twisting with anger and bitterness, she spat at her brother, 'Oh, yes, the classic trick—lead me on until I say something really out of order! And is it all now round the bloody village? That—oh, how wonderful—the McMahons have a new little relative, titter, titter...'

'No! No one knows but me!' Ellie exclaimed. 'And I'm *not* a relative!' Swinging round on Feargal, she said desperately, 'Tell her!'

'Tell her what? That you aren't a money-grubbing little cheat? That you aren't here to blackmail someone? That you didn't lie? Or that you aren't a relative?'

Staring at him, her beautiful eyes reflecting her unhappiness and hurt, she wondered if the whole family was warped by suspicion. Or was it only Feargal and his half-sister? Her face white, she whispered, 'But I didn't do any of those things—you know I didn't.'

'And did your grandmother send you forth with her blessing?' Phena asked waspishly, diverting her attention.

'Grandmother? What has she got to do with anything?'

'Oh, a great deal, I should think. She was the one who refused to let me see my father.'

'What?'

'Oh, yes; don't pretend you don't know about that juicy bit of gossip,' she spat bitterly.

'You did go to see him? When you were in England?'

'Oh, yes. For all the good it did me.'

'Did you tell her who you were?'

'Of course.'

Oh hell. 'And what did she say?'

'You know her; what do you think she said?'

'Get off my doorstep?'

'Something like that,' she admitted with her twisted smile.

Yes, of course she had, because Grandmother had known full well that her husband could never have fathered a child. And she could well imagine how scathing she would have been. Understanding, or at least in part, she murmured, 'And so, because you've been hurt, are angry, think I'm somehow privileged, you want me to be hurt...' The sudden, loud slam of the front door, and the sound of raised voices made her break off.

'Oh, God. Now what?' Feargal breathed. Motioning them both to silence, he walked to the door and looked out. Turning back, his strong face set in harsh lines that made him look older, he instructed coldly, 'Not one word of this will be breathed to Mother. Now out, both of you.' When they'd moved past him, he quietly closed the bedroom door.

Standing on the landing, the sound of Terry's tearful voice floated up to them. She'd collected her wedding dress, and it wasn't what she wanted; it didn't fit properly, and the woman in Drogheda who had made it had gone away on holiday, and her assistant didn't know anything about it, and wasn't a seamstress, so now what the hell was she supposed to do? The wedding was off, because no way was she going to walk down the aisle looking like an eejit!

And Rose, who chose that inopportune moment to walk out of the lounge, began wringing her hands and saying wasn't it a judgement on them all? Mrs McMahon offered inadequate comfort and made bad worse by saying she was sure it looked lovely and not to be so silly. Terry told her she was a fool and that if she couldn't see it looked like someone's frilly bedspread then she must be blind. And Mrs McMahon who naturally hadn't seen it because hadn't she just this minute arrived back from the village and wasn't the dress still in its bag, looked up at the three hovering on the stairs as though it were a divine deliverance, mumbled vaguely about a headache coming on, and thankfully abandoned her responsibilities to whoever was willing to take them on.

'Oh, Feargal, what am I to do?' Terry wailed as her brother walked lightly down the stairs.

'Find another dressmaker,' he said calmly as though it were the most natural thing in the world to have a wedding dress that didn't fit on the eve of the great day.

'Don't be daft! No other dressmaker will take on someone else's work!'

Unconscious arrogance in every line of him, he raised one eyebrow in astonishment. 'Of course they will.'

'They won't,' she stormed, in no mood to be comforted. 'And anyway, there isn't time!'

'There's always time. I'll get someone to come here.'

'Of course he will!' Phena injected sarcastically. 'Can't the great Feargal McMahon do anything?'

'Phena,' Feargal warned without raising his voice. 'Be quiet.'

'Oh, yes, let it be Phena who has to shut up! Why the hell should I expect anything else? *I'm* not a proper member of the family!' Descending the last few stairs, she turned on her elegantly shod heel, and walked off towards the kitchen.

'Now look what you've done,' Mrs McMahon moaned.

Ellie, a silent watcher, and still hurting from all the accusations being hurled around upstairs, and who wasn't exactly known for her commanding presence, took one look at Terry's tear-stained face, and offered quietly, 'Will you let me have a look?'

The glance of astonishment Feargal gave her should have made her back off, but she was so thoroughly fed up with this family, with being the meat in the sandwich of everyone's feud, that she ignored him. Ducking past Feargal, she took Terry's arm, and urged her towards the stairs.

'Rose, will you make some tea, please? And then bring some up to Terry's room?'

'But I have all the rooms to get ready for the guests that are arriving...'

'Rose,' Feargal put in coldly. 'Make the tea.' Turning to his sister, he instructed, 'Let me know if you need me to find a dressmaker.'

'All right; thanks, Feargal. Come on, Ellie,' she finished miserably.

Leading the way up to Terry's room, fervently wishing she'd left this madhouse when she'd had the chance, Ellie stood back for Terry to enter first.

Unzipping the long bag, Terry hung the white frothy dress on the outside of the wardrobe then stared at it depressingly. 'It makes me look like a cake!' she pronounced dramatically.

'Well, put it on and let me see.'

With a total lack of enthusiasm, Terry stripped down to her bra and pants and, climbed apathetically into the dress. 'There! You see? It's awful!'

Leaning back against the wall, her arms folded, Ellie stared at it critically. 'It isn't that the dress is awful,' she finally pronounced. 'It's that it doesn't suit you. If we took off all the frills, altered the neck, took the waist in a tiny bit...' Walking across to her, she turned her to look in the full-length mirror. Flattening down the awful frills, her head on one side, she asked, 'See?' Then, holding the excess material at the back of Terry's waist, giving the dress a longer, more elegant line, she murmured, 'What do you think?'

A frantic look in her eyes, as though removing the frills would somehow diminish her, make her less than lovely on her special day, Terry gave a little murmur of distress.

'If I take them off carefully, and you don't like it without, we can always put them back...' Ellie encouraged. 'But without them it will look much better, I promise, and if we take out these awful shoulder-pads...'

With a gesture of defeat, Terry exclaimed, 'Oh, do it, then! I don't care!'

'Yes, you do, of course you do,' Ellie said gently. 'Now come on. Positive thinking, that's the thing.'

Helping her out of the dress, she threw it across the bed. 'Right; scissors? Thread?'

'In Mother's workbox,' Terry said listlessly as she eyed the frothy creation on the bed. 'It didn't seem to look like that when I had the fitting.'

'No,' Ellie agreed comfortingly. But the dressmaker had obviously decided it was too plain and added a few frills to liven it up a bit. A definite mistake. She might wander round looking like a ragbag herself, but the look suited her, and anyway she was one of those fortunate people who could wear anything, even an old sack, and look beautiful. Terry, who was taller, and far more slender, would look much better in classic lines. Frills and furbelows just made her look stupid.

Incarcerated in Terry's room, they made do with sandwiches for dinner, and endless cups of tea. Terry sat looking anxious while Ellie carefully unpicked, altered, moved all the tiny buttons that ran down the back, rearranged the small bustle, put little tucks into the bustline to make it fit more snugly. She made Terry try it on, take it off, changed something else, and finally, at gone midnight, she had done all that she could do, and only then did she allow Terry to look at herself in the mirror.

'There. What do you think?'

Terry didn't look as though she knew what to think. She looked absolutely staggered. 'Oh, Ellie,' she whispered as she twisted to and fro to get a better look. 'It doesn't even seem like the same dress!'

'No,' Ellie agreed with a small smile. It looked altogether better. 'Where are the shoes you're going to wear?'

'In the wardrobe.'

'Then get them and put them on!'

'Oh, right,' she said sheepishly. Collecting them, and slipping her feet inside, Terry looked again at her reflection.

'Head-dress?'

Pointing to the box on the bed, she continued to stare at herself as though she couldn't believe it was her.

Eyeing the seed-pearl head-dress with the fly-away veil, Ellie determinedly picked up the scissors and cut all the net off.

'What are you doing?' Terry exclaimed in horror.

'You'll see.' Rescuing a piece of the frill from the dress, Ellie cut it to the shape she wanted, attached it with pins to the back of the headband, laid it down, picked up Terry's brush, backcombed the other girl's hair so that it stood further out from her head, giving a similarity of the style she thought she should have, carefully arranged the head-dress, and turned Terry back to the mirror. 'Like that!' she said confidently.

'Oh. Oh, Ellie, I look lovely.'

'Yes, you do. Go and show your mother... Oh, no, better not,' she argued as she caught sight of the time.

'Yes, of course I must! She won't be asleep yet. And, oh, Ellie, if you hadn't been here, I'd have gone down the aisle looking such a fright...' Rushing across the room, she gave Ellie a warm hug. 'Sure and wasn't it an act of God that you came at all?' Picking up her skirts, she hurried out and along to her mother's room. Trailing after her, Ellie stood on the landing, and listened. An act of God? She was beginning to think it was the wish of the devil. Hearing her praises lavishly extolled, she gave a sad, wry smile and returned to Terry's room to clear up. She could sew the veil on properly in the morning, before she left.

'Well, well,' Feargal drawled from the doorway, 'aren't we the clever one.'

With a long sigh, she turned to face him. 'Not now, Feargal. I'm too tired for verbal duelling.'

'Are you?'

'Yes.' The needlework box clutched to her chest, she added, 'And didn't you want Terry to look the best she possibly could on her wedding day?'

'Naturally.'

'But not that it should be me who made it so. Well, I find I don't care any more...'

'Meaning you did care before?' he asked silkily.

Oh, what the hell did it matter now? 'Yes,' she agreed, 'meaning that I did before. I liked you. Very much. Happy now? Now that you've been proved right?'

'Ecstatic.'

'Good, then there's nothing more to say. Goodnight, Feargal,' she said dismissively.

Turning away, he walked along to his own room.

Enough was more than enough. And shouldn't she have known? All relationships turned to ashes sooner or later. Perhaps there was something wrong in her make-up. Perhaps she didn't have enough cuddles as a child. Oh, Gramps, she thought tiredly, what a nice little legacy you left your granddaughter.

Before Terry came back, she went along to her own room and thankfully closed the door. Picking Gwen Bear up from the bed, and hugging the soft toy to her for comfort, she stood at the window and stared out at the cloudy night sky. No point in thinking about it any more, no point in any of it really. Gramps was dead, and could no longer be hurt. Her parents weren't likely to find out... Only Mrs McMahon could still be affected—and she had asked her to keep it a secret. She must have loved the real father of Phena very much if she was willing to put up with all of this. Feargal's censure, Phena's bitterness—a hell of a burden to carry all your adult life. And it must be a burden, knowing that your family thought you a cheat, knowing that you had hurt them, and would continue to hurt them until you died. Ellie didn't think she would have had that sort of courage. And in the morning she would pack up and quietly leave, would never see this disturbing family again.

Disappointment that Feargal wasn't the man she had thought him had been replaced by a sadness for things not to be. You could look at someone and like them, be excited, hopeful, and then, in the wink of an eye, it could all turn to dust. Replacing Gwen Bear on the quilt, she got ready for bed.

When she woke in the morning, she felt a profound reluctance to meet any of the family in case she got drawn into any more dramas. They certainly seemed to

thrive on them. It might be nice, mightn't it, to get back
home and resume her quiet ordinary life? A relief, certainly. No one to accuse her, misunderstand. After re-
packing her case, she fervently hoped for the last time,
she had a wash, and because it looked sunny and warm
outside dressed in a skimpy vest with a blouse over the
top, and a rather strange Fifties-style skirt covered in
poppies. She would have some breakfast, she decided,
and then get away. Unfortunately, as she descended the
stairs, she heard raised voices from the study. Phena
and Feargal. Even more unfortunately, the study door
was open, and as she tried to get past without being seen
Phena stormed out.

'Still here?' she asked nastily.

'Only for a few minutes. I shall be leaving as soon as
I've had something to eat. And settled up with your
brother for my board and lodging,' she added hastily.

'Huh!' Pushing rudely past Ellie, she stalked upstairs.

Deciding she might as well get it over and done with,
and indeed settle up, she took a deep breath, and pushed
the study door wide.

'What do you want?' he asked, every bit as rude as
his sister.

'To settle up.' Taking her cheque-book from her bag,
she stood waiting.

With a derisive smile, he leaned back in his chair.
'You do it so well, don't you?' he asked admiringly.

'Do what so well?'

'Come now, Ellie, you really mustn't continue to hide
your talents. They're so prodigious.'

'Yes, they are, aren't they? Unfortunately, you seem
to have them by the wrong end, but, seeing as no
amount of protestations will make you change your

mind, I shan't bother. And,' she tacked on, 'it is my profound hope that I shall never see any of you ever again.'

'You think it isn't mine?' Returning to his former position, he picked up his pen. 'While you're eating your last breakfast, I'll make out your bill,' he concluded dismissively.

'Thank you. Money is always better than experience, isn't it?' she couldn't resist taunting.

'Usually. In my sadly jaundiced view, experience comes very expensive. Certainly it has in this case. One way or another, you seem to have cost me a great deal. Phena thinks recent developments entitle her to a newer, bigger house, which she expects me to pay for, with pleasure, despite the fact that the wedding is already running into a fortune. But Terry is happy. She now has a wedding dress that cost me the national debt, but which now bears no relation to the original creation because all the expensive seed-pearls are strewn around her bedroom floor, and which the dog thought would be marvellous to eat and is now residing at the local vet's and which will cost me even more money. So, you see, little Miss Ellie Browne with an "E", why I decided that I no longer wish to put it down to experience.'

Before she could reply, even if she'd known what to say, Phena sauntered back in. 'Not gone yet?' she taunted before turning to her brother. 'I forgot to mention refurnishing. You will take that into account, won't you?' she asked sweetly.

'No. Now go away, I'm busy.'

'Aren't we all, dear?' Turning to Ellie, she gave her a false smile. 'Those who get the luck get the responsibility. That's only fair, isn't it?'

'Luck?' Ellie queried. 'It doesn't sound as though he has any luck at all!'

'He got the farm, didn't he? And the house, and everything that was going?'

And his mother, and you, and Terry and her problems, and now herself.

'But little Ellie Browne isn't going to be given a chance to be a part of it,' she murmured with mock sorrow.

'No, but then Ellie Browne didn't want to be a part of it in the first place. And I am not little.'

'No? But poor, hm, Ellie?' With a disparaging look down at her clothes, Phena smiled. 'Yes, definitely poor. Such a pity, because Mother was so taken with you, wasn't she?'

'Your mother has been very kind,' Ellie said stiffly.

'Well, she would be, wouldn't she? You're the granddaughter of her—lover. Had some nice little chats, did you?' she purred with a delicate arch of one eyebrow. 'Lots of little confidences exchanged?' Returning her attention to her brother, who had remained a silent spectator throughout their exchange, she asked, 'Heard from Huw?'

'Yes,' he said curtly, 'he'll be here tomorrow.'

'Oh, what a shame Ellie won't be here to meet yet another member of our delightful family. A legitimate one at that. She'd have liked Huw. Very susceptible to a pretty face, is Huw.'

'Phena...' Feargal put in warningly. 'Leave it.'

'Why should I? Just because there's no stigma attached to your name, or Huw's, or Terry's...'

'There is no stigma—or only in your mind. Ellie, leave us,' he added coldly. It wasn't a request.

Only too happy to oblige, she slipped out and along to the kitchen for her breakfast. She doubted she would ever be in danger of taking anyone at face value again, not after meeting Feargal and his sister. A chip on her shoulder, did he say? It was a damned great boulder.

When she'd finished eating—not that she'd felt very hungry—she went in search of Mrs McMahon in order to say goodbye again. She was nowhere in the house. Rose said she'd seen her walking in the direction of the milking sheds, and with a little nod Ellie went out into the grounds. It was a beautiful day, the sun shining, birds singing . . . It would have been more appropriate to leave in rain. Passing the two horses that had looked so sad and bedraggled that first day, she lingered to watch them. Leaning on the fence, her chin on her arms, she sighed. She'd arrived in Slane with such high hopes, expected to bring pleasure to someone, and all she'd done was cause trouble.

'Praying for a miracle?'

Swinging round, she stared at Phena. A Phena who looked as though she might have been crying. 'No, just looking for your mother to say goodbye.' And then on impulse Ellie laid her hand compassionately on the other woman's. 'Phena, I'm sorry about the letters. I truly had no knowledge of what they contained when I brought them. Didn't know about you, or your mother, or anything. I never meant for any of this to happen.'

'Didn't you?' Moving her arm, so that Ellie's hand fell away, she stepped back.

'No, and I'm sorry you're so bitter about it all, but truly it was none of my doing.' Searching Phena's face for a response, and finding none, she sighed.

Turning away, intending to resume her search for Mrs McMahon, Phena asked, 'How much did he leave you?'

'Who?' she asked, puzzled. 'Grandfather?'

'Of course Grandfather,' she mimicked.

'Not very much, just enough to enable me to come to Ireland.'

'Oh, left to your parents, was it? But it will come to you eventually, won't it?'

'What will? There wasn't very much to leave. The house, I suppose, but that's about all. You weren't done out of anything, Phena. Really you weren't. And money isn't everything. You have a loving family; that's more than a lot of people get.'

'Is it? And how would you know?' The bitterness on her face made her look ugly as she turned and walked away, back to the house.

Was that how she would have felt if she'd been in her position? Ellie honestly didn't know. With a sad shake of her head she walked on towards the farm buildings.

Peering into the milking sheds, she hastily ducked out when she saw Feargal, his shirt off, fiddling with a piece of machinery. Good God, the whole family were like blasted jack-in-the-boxes. You only had to turn round, and another one popped up. He must have left the study shortly after herself, and practically sprinted up here.

'Looking for me?'

With a defeated sigh, she turned back. 'No, for your mother.' He was very brown, she thought inconsequentially as he strolled towards her, and quite devastatingly attractive. He was wiping his hands on his shirt.

'Don't do that,' she reproved without thinking. 'Use a rag.'

His eyebrows went up, and she flushed. 'Have a nice little chat with Phena, did you?'

'No, just apologised for causing her any trouble.'

'Trouble?' With a cynical little laugh, he leaned his shoulder against the side of the shed. 'And you'd know all about that, wouldn't you, Ellie?'

Staring at him, into blue, blue eyes that she had once found so attractive, she shook her head tiredly. 'Did you work out how much I owe you?'

Bright mockery filled his face, and he gave a slow smile. It wasn't a nice smile. Not wickedly attractive like before, but dangerous. 'Do you know, if I didn't dislike you so much, I would be full of admiration?'

'Feargal, just tell me how much I owe you.'

'All those lies, without batting an eyelid...'

'I did not lie!'

'So what did you say to Phena just now?'

'I told you! She looked as though she'd been crying, and I felt sorry—'

'Dear God,' he interrupted, 'no wonder you get away with murder, eyes so wide one would swear you were innocent. A face devoid of guile, the sweetest smile I've ever seen. Sorry for her, were you?'

'Yes! I can understand her bitterness—'

'Oh, can you?'

'Yes! And will you stop keep interrupting me?' she ordered furiously. 'And to blame me for her bitterness is the height of absurdity! She was bitter before I ever came on the scene!'

'But not quite so mercenary, and I find it exceedingly distasteful for you to arrogantly assume you might understand my sister a great deal better than I ever could. I do *not* need your input on the subject. I do *not* need your understanding, or your damned sorrow!

What I need from you, Ellie Browne,' he uttered distastefully, 'is for you to get the hell out of my life!'

'Which I will do as soon as you tell me how much I owe!'

Staring at her, he asked quietly, 'You really want to pay?'

'Yes!' she insisted, and to her utter alarm and astonishment he caught her arm and pulled her towards the nearby barn.

'Just so we won't be seen,' he said silkily.

Trying to drag her arm free, she gritted, 'And why don't we want to be seen?'

'Because, by my reckoning, payment tends to get more than a little physical.'

'Payment gets a... Are you out of your mind? Let me go this minute!'

'No.'

Digging her heels in, she glared at him. She might only lose her temper about once every five years, but when she lost it, boy, did she lose it, and events these last few days had been urging her dangerously near to boiling-point. Squinting her eyes, because the contrast from bright day to the deep shadow in the barn made it difficult to see where she was going, and wary of stumbling and falling over, she grabbed at the doorframe, and shot out her foot to trip him up. He recovered far more quickly than she would have thought possible for such a big man, but the drag on her arm nearly pulled it out of its socket. Biting her lip to stop herself crying out, she stared at him bitterly. She might not have been able to see his expression, but she could definitely see his smile—and it wasn't a very nice one. But then neither was hers.

Moving back towards her, slowly, and his physical strength being the greater, he easily prised her fingers loose, and before she could recover he pushed her off balance and into a pile of hay. Hands on hips, he stood staring down at her, and his wide grin said it all. 'Want to fight?'

'No,' she denied stonily. 'Leave.'

'Which you will, when I've had the truth.'

Her face set, she struggled into a sitting position. Deliberately ignoring him, she began to pick straw out of her clothes, and only when she was satisfied that she had removed every last one, and had taken in all there was to take in about her immediate surroundings, did she look up at him. 'What truth would you like?' she asked nicely.

'The truth about why you came. And I should perhaps warn you, Ellie, that in game-playing I always win. Always,' he emphasised.

'Really? Not familiar with the maxim that pride goeth before a fall, Feargal?'

'Oh, yes,' he agreed softly. 'My pride, your fall.'

With a snort of derision, she got slowly to her feet. 'And if you push me down again,' she warned quietly, 'you might very well find that you have a tiger by the tail. I might be "little",' she parodied, 'but we English are noted for our belief in fighting to the last blood-filled ditch.'

'You think the Irish aren't?'

'Yes,' she agreed kindly, 'but temper is usually your downfall.'

'Don't judge the one by the many, Ellie,' he warned softly, 'because you're likely to come seriously unstuck.'

'You think so?' All the while she had been talking, she had been moving little by little to one side, her movements casual, and when she was exactly where she wanted to be she reached out and grasped, lifted, and swiftly jabbed the pitchfork that had been standing in the corner of the stall.

Quick as she was, Feargal was quicker and swerved swiftly to one side. The fork missed him by centimetres. And instead of the anger, retribution she had been expecting, and the stance she had adopted to prevent, he gave an exuberant laugh. 'You think I should equip myself with a similar implement and we could have a duel?' Grinning like an idiot, he grabbed up the lid of the bran tub, and proceeded to defend himself.

'Oh, you think you're so clever, don't you?' she gritted. Goaded beyond endurance, she took a wild swing that connected with his shield with such force that it nearly wrenched her arms out of their sockets. Muttering imprecations, she recovered her balance and swung the unwieldy implement the other way, and the more he laughed, the angrier she got. Jabbing violently forward, with no thought whatsoever of what she would do if she actually hit him, she didn't even notice where he was retreating until it was too late. Her face grimly determined, she lunged, and in one swift movement he tossed his shield aside, grabbed the pitchfork, and pulled. Off balance, she had to release her grip in order to save herself, and before she knew what he was about he had tossed the pitchfork into the next stall, and kicked her feet out from under her.

Following her down, he knelt across her thighs, grabbed her wrists in his strong hands and held them out one each side. 'Now what?' he taunted. 'Black magic? A swift spell?'

Out of breath, and furious to note that he wasn't even panting, she struggled to free herself, then glared at him. 'Get off!' she spat.

'No, so now let's have the truth,' he encouraged. 'All about how you knew about us before you left England. All about how you persuaded Donal to introduce us.'

'Donal?' she scoffed. 'I didn't even know Donal. I'd met him once.'

'Once is enough for him to be of use. And then, once we had met, all you had to do was arrive at my home, exclaiming, "Surprise, surprise!" and use your little lever to gain entry into my family.'

'And you really think I'm stupid enough to believe that—what was it, blackmail?—would get me the very thing you think I desire? Entry into your family? How very arrogant you are, Feargal, and might I remind you that it was you who sought me out, not the other way round?'

'True, but only because Donal had done his ground-work. It's really rather clever when you think about it.'

'Certainly, it would be extraordinarily clever if it were true—and if one had ever thought you were the sort of man to be manipulated. Which of course you aren't. Mind, I suppose if I were the sort of person you obviously think I am I would have known about your pre-dilection for pretty girls—and your low boredom threshold,' she said scathingly. 'But what I really don't understand is why on earth you should think anyone of a sound mind would actually want to gain entry into your very confusing family!'

'Because the very confusing family is wealthy? And by your own admission you are broke—and, also by your admission, your mother wants you to marry someone sophisticated, wealthy... True?'

'True. And you think my parents are also in on the plot?'

'Perhaps. Your father paid for your trip to Dublin, which you yourself admitted was unheard of.'

'And if it were all true, do you really think I would have admitted it? If I'm clever enough to plot out something so absurd, don't you think I would be clever enough to conceal it? No, Feargal, it won't wash. I told you the truth.'

'And I'm really expected to believe that Donal, of his own bat, sent me to Wexford to meet you, knowing you were about to seek out my family, just to be friendly? And that by a stroke of coincidence no bed and breakfasts were open and you were forced to seek help at the Hall? The very house where the woman you were looking for lived? Try again, Ellie.'

'No,' she denied coldly. 'No more tries, no more explanations. I told the truth.'

'And have now come out to the barn to convince me of it? To convince me that you are in fact the sweet, simple little soul you'd have everyone believe?'

'That would be pretty arrogant of me, wouldn't it? I'm not so certain of my charms. I came out to find your mother, I told you, to say goodbye. As far as I knew you were still in the study.'

'But I'd just seen you talking to Phena, who told you I wasn't in the study,' he said softly.

With a sound of disgust in the back of her throat, she derided, 'For an intelligent man, you're being incredibly stupid—and conceited,' she tacked on, 'if you think every woman you ever run across wants to trap you, or gain entry into your family,' she mocked.

'And is this the real Ellie Browne? The girl with the tart tongue? And a face that is suddenly hard?'

'No, no more than the real Feargal McMahon is the oaf sitting across me arguing himself into a corner.'

'Oaf?'

'Yes.'

'You didn't think so once.'

'No, but then I didn't know you, did I?'

'Still don't, Ellie Browne,' he said softly. 'Still don't.' And, much to her alarm, he suddenly leaned forward.

CHAPTER SEVEN

THE SHIFT in Feargal's body brought awareness which Ellie determinedly ignored—brought warmth, and she gritted her teeth to deny it.

'And whatever your reasons,' he continued with cold precision, 'whatever your motives, it doesn't alter the fact that you've caused my family a lot of grief. Phena, despite her odd ways, does not deserve to be hurt further, does not deserve to have it all dragged up and dissected.'

'You think I don't know that? And I'd like to know how many damned times I'm supposed to tell you that I had no motives either!' Ellie retorted.

'And my mother,' he continued crisply as though she had not spoken, 'did not need reminding of things that are best left forgotten.'

'And, for the fifty-fifth time, I did not know! But what I dearly would like to know is why you're always so damned suspicious!'

'Because you're not the first. Admittedly the others weren't nearly so beguiling, or inventive, and do you know what is worse?' he derided himself mockingly. 'The fact that, knowing you as I do, knowing what you have deliberately done, I still find you attractive.'

'Well, isn't that a shame! I'm glad to say I don't feel the same.'

'Liar. And it would be such a pity to waste all that femininity, wouldn't it? All that plotting and planning.'

'No, it wouldn't be a pity at all! It would be an enormous relief—and if you're waiting for me to struggle, demand you release me, you can wait till hell freezes over, Feargal McMahon, because I wouldn't give you the satisfaction!'

'No? But there are other kinds of satisfaction, aren't there?'

Hanging on to her temper, and, it had to be admitted, her rioting feelings, with an effort, she retorted, 'To someone like you, perhaps. Not to me.' Unbearably aware of the warmth of his body resting against hers, and wishing to hell she wasn't, wishing that mere strength of mind would negate it, she held him stare for stare.

'Beautiful Ellie. Beautiful lying Ellie. There's a sexual excitement about confrontations like this, isn't there?'

'No,' she denied stonily.

'No?' His voice was soft, silky, which she supposed was a warning, but she still wasn't prepared for the speed with which he moved her top aside.

'Don't,' she gritted, trying to put it back in place and only succeeding in entering into an undignified struggle.

'Don't?' he taunted. 'When it was what you wanted all along? Why else go braless?'

'Not for your damned benefit! I often go without one! And don't do that!' she cried thickly as his thumb moved on her exposed breast. 'God, I hate you!'

'Liar.'

Her mouth tight, her breathing more than a little erratic, she wrenched his thumb away and dragged the abused material of her top back over her breast.

With a wolfish smile, he grabbed her wrist again and put it above her head with the other one, and then slowly, deliberately slowly, bent towards her mouth. 'Stop pretending it isn't what you want,' he breathed as his lips touched hers.

I'm not! she wanted to shout, but suddenly didn't have the breath. And it wasn't fair! It really wasn't fair. If he'd hurt her, used force, she could have fought back, but he didn't, just used a gentle persuasive movement that unlocked her lips, parted her teeth. She could have struggled, but it wouldn't have gained her anything; he was too strong, or so she told herself. But she didn't respond—at least she didn't do that!—or only a little bit, only the very smallest bit, because it was so very sweet, so very exciting, so very much what she had always hoped a kiss might be, and if he believed it was what she wanted, why not let him think so? She was the one who gained by the exquisite experience, wasn't she? It would be something to remember, wouldn't it? That once she had been capable of responding? Capable of desire? Even his strong hands holding hers captive weren't hurting; on the contrary, even that manacle was exciting because his thumbs were slowly stroking the insides of her wrists, sending shafts of awareness along her arms to her body, which was growing warm, soft, as though inviting his to sink further against her, into her... No! As sanity returned, she gave a little jerk and wrenched her mouth free. 'No!' she said thickly.

With a laugh deep in his throat, he opened his eyes wide. 'No?'

'No. And to use your sexuality as a weapon is despicable!' she spat. 'Demeaning. You know what effect you have on women, and you—you shamelessly use it!'

'Mm. And are you seriously trying to tell me that women don't use the same weapons? Shamelessly?' he mocked.

'I'm not telling you anything at all! Now get off me! I don't like being used.'

'You loved being used,' he corrected with his hateful smile. 'Your skin is warm and flushed, your heart beating fast—and you want me.'

'Might have wanted you—in different circumstances.'

With a disbelieving smile, he released her and got slowly to his feet. 'In any circumstances,' he corrected. With a smile that was no longer mocking, or even amused, he said, 'Call the debt cancelled. And by the time I get back to the house I expect you to be gone.'

'Willingly!' she snapped.

'And if I ever hear of any little tales being put about concerning Phena, or any of my family...'

'You'll what?' she derided bravely.

'Make you pay,' he said softly. Collecting up his shirt, he sauntered out into the sunshine.

Bastard. Magnificent, infuriating, cynical bastard. Scrambling to her feet, she set herself to rights, before stalking back to the house. Hurrying up to her room, she grabbed up her things, and stormed down to where her car was parked. Opening the boot, she flung everything in, slammed it, and climbed behind the wheel.

If he thought she would stay one more minute in his house, to be insulted, mauled... Twisting the key in the ignition, she wished, belatedly, that she'd struggled more in the barn, been more scathing... In fact now she was away from him she could think of a hundred and one things she should have said—done—and what the hell was the matter with this damned car? Taking the key out, and looking at it, as though it might have changed without her knowledge, she jabbed it back in and twisted violently. Nothing. Not even a splutter.

The door was opened beside her and she gave a nervous start.

'Trouble?' Feargal drawled. 'My, my, it just doesn't seem to be your day, does it?'

'Oh, shut up! Try being useful for a change and find out what the hell is wrong with it!'

'Please?' he prompted mockingly.

'Please,' she said through her teeth.

Leaning his arms along the top of the car, he stared down at her. 'But you know what's wrong with it, and it really won't work, Ellie.'

'I do not know what's wrong with it!' she gritted.

With a disbelieving shrug, he walked round to release the bonnet, and then glanced into the engine. 'My, my, such wilful damage. I do hope you know how to repair it, Ellie, otherwise you will be backpacking out of here.'

'What?' she asked blankly. Swinging herself hastily out of the car, she slammed the door.

'Temper, temper,' he mocked.

'Oh, go play in the traffic!' Going to stand beside him, she too peered into the engine. 'What's that wire doing loose?' she demanded.

'Waving?'

'Feargal,' she warned, and was aware of him slowly turning to face her. Glancing at him, she saw him frown. 'Well?'

'Feargal?'

Peering round the raised bonnet, she stared at Terry who was beckoning her brother urgently from the open front door. 'Feargal! I need to talk to you a minute! Urgently!'

With a last glance at Ellie, he strolled towards his sister.

Ellie couldn't actually hear what they were saying, only that they seemed to be arguing. Heatedly. Then, with a sound of disgust, Feargal pushed past her and went into the house. With a sheepish look, Terry descended the steps and came to stand by Ellie.

'I did it,' she confessed.

'What?'

'Disabled the car. I want you to stay for my wedding!' she said strenuously. 'After you did my dress and all, were so nice, it isn't fair! And I want you to stay! It's my day, after all! And I can have who I want,' she finished determinedly.

'Oh, Terry!' Ellie exclaimed helplessly. 'I can't stay, really I can't.'

'Yes, you can! Mother wants you to stay too! And anyway, Feargal said it's all right!'

Oh, I just bet he did.

'Please?' she pleaded. 'It's only one more day. And Feargal will be out on the farm, you won't need to see him—please?'

'No,' she denied obdurately. 'Come on, Terry, just mend it and let me get out of here.'

'I can't!' she said with a triumphant grin. 'Declan told me how to disable it, but not how to mend it. Feargal can do it later,' she shrugged. 'Come on.'

Her mouth compressed, Ellie sighed. 'Then I will have to walk down to the village and find a mechanic at the garage.'

Her face crumpling, Terry asked wistfully, 'You don't want to stay?'

'It's not a question of want! Oh, Terry, don't do this to me.'

'But I like you! Now come on, stop being silly.' Without waiting for an answer, she walked round to the boot and began to take out the luggage.

'Terry...'

'Don't be cross,' Terry pleaded. 'Did you really not want to stay for my wedding?'

'Yes, of course, but Terry...'

'Feargal will be all right, honest.'

God, the whole family seemed to have learned manipulation from the cradle. And would Feargal now believe she had engineered this? Of course he would.

'Want to come into Drogheda with me?' Terry wheedled.

'How?' Ellie asked drily.

'On the bus, of course. Come on, it will be fun. You can view the severed head of St Oliver Plunkett in St Peter's Church.'

'Oh, thank you so much! That sounds entirely delightful! Just what I need right at the present moment!'

With a giggle, Terry helped her carry her luggage back to her room, then dragged her back downstairs and along to the village to wait for the bus. Well, she supposed it would keep her out of Feargal's orbit. Pity it wasn't his severed head she was going to view!

Actually she quite enjoyed the day, saw things through Terry's eyes with a different perspective, and was astonished all over again at how warm and friendly everyone was. And in between Terry's forays into various shops did indeed view the bizarre remains in St Peter's Church. Terry seemed to regard it with awe and wonder, Ellie thought it was desperate, morbid, the stuff of nightmares. And if Feargal had his way he'd probably like to see her head there in its place.

When they returned to the house, Terry tried to persuade her to accompany her to visit one of her girlfriends, for a sort of hen night, she supposed, but Ellie pleaded tiredness and went up to her room, and that, except for a brief trip to the kitchen for something to eat, was where she stayed. She heard the guests arriving, noisy, laughing, and she stupidly felt excluded, lonely. She didn't ever remember feeling lonely before, left out. She knew it was mostly to do with Feargal's behaviour, and her own shaming enjoyment of it. Lying on her bed, trying to read a book, she watched the time tick round until it was a reasonable time to get undressed and try to sleep. One more day, and this time, finally, she would leave.

THE NEXT MORNING dawned with the chaos usually associated with weddings, whether organised or not, and which left Ellie no time to think. Which was perhaps just as well. There seemed to be a veritable army of helpers needed to open up the big downstairs rooms, and wherever she went there seemed yet another one poised to ask her a question she was unable to answer. The caterers arrived too early and got in the way of the woman who was doing the flowers. The guests with a morning to waste until the ceremony at two o'clock got under everyone's feet. Terry appeared to be having a nervous breakdown; her mother was foolishly trying to be everything to everybody and only succeeded in adding to the confusion. By contrast, Phena seemed intent on avoiding everyone, and anyone who did deign to speak to her got snapped at for their trouble.

Huw, a brown-eyed version of Feargal himself, accompanied by a pretty little blonde girl, looked as though he might enjoy causing chaos just for the hell of it. Of Feargal she saw no sign.

The dog got over-excited and took exception to one of the chefs and had to be shut in the barn where he howled mournfully enough to wake the dead. And one of the bridesmaids didn't turn up.

Mrs McMahon felt herself incapable of assisting Terry to dress because it had only just burst upon her that it was her daughter getting married and she would leave and never be seen again. Rose and Mary were for once showing a united front and refused to leave the kitchen because they didn't quite like the way the young women from the town who had come to be waitresses were poking and prying into their cupboards with their noses in the air. The bridesmaid eventually turned up with a tale as long as her arm as to why, which nobody listened to. The various relations didn't have time to help the bride because they had to get themselves ready, and when Ellie knocked on Terry's door to offer her own help she found the bride-to-be face down on the bed in floods of tears.

'And wouldn't you think just one person would be glad to help me?' she wailed when Ellie asked what on earth was the matter. 'It will all go wrong, I know it will. And I can't find Feargal...'

'No, he appears to be the only one with any sense,' Ellie said drily.

With a hiccuping sob, Terry rolled over and sat up. 'Oh, don't say that; it's supposed to be my special day.'

'It is your special day,' Ellie soothed. Perching on the edge of the bed, she smiled at the woebegone girl. 'And won't they all feel terrible about it when they stop to think what they're doing to you?' she asked in a fair imitation of an Irish brogue.

'Oh, Ellie!' Terry exclaimed with a tearful smile. 'A voice of sanity amid all the chaos.'

'Well, that makes a change. Come on, go and have your shower.'

When Terry was ready, and everyone had been in to have a look, exclaim, and, in the case of Terry's mother, cry, she ushered them all downstairs to wait for the cars. She felt exhausted. Returning to Terry's room, she smiled. 'All right?'

'Yes, I'm fine now. Do I look OK?'

'Lovely,' Ellie promised. 'Radiant and beautiful. Nerves all gone now?'

'Yes,' she admitted softly as she continued to stare at herself in the full-length mirror. 'I feel all sort of calm and—happy.' Turning to face Ellie, she smiled, said, 'I can't thank you enough for all you've done...' and only then seemed to realise that Ellie herself wasn't all dressed up. 'Oh, Ellie, you'll miss it!' she exclaimed in distress. 'Go quickly and get ready.'

'No,' she said gently. 'I'll wait here for you all to come back.'

'Oh, but, Ellie...'

'Honestly, I'd much rather. I don't have anything to wear to the church. Not a hat or anything. I'll wait here and make sure it's all ready for when you get back.'

'But didn't you want to see it?' Terry asked, sounding so disappointed that Ellie hastily reassured her.

'Yes, of course I did—and I can pop down to the church and see you come out,' she offered impulsively, which thankfully seemed to satisfy the other girl.

'Oh, all right. Is Feargal ready?'

'I don't know. Shall I go—?' The soft knock at the door made her break off. 'That's probably him now.' Staring at the door, Ellie seemed quite unable to tear her eyes away as it slowly opened and Feargal walked in. He looked cool and composed, and quite devastatingly attractive. He looked as though he'd stepped from the pages of a history book. The rakish hero. His dark hair had been trimmed and lay tidily against the high collar of the grey, swallow-tailed suit jacket. The darker grey cravat made his eyes look bluer, his skin more tanned. The narrow trousers made his legs look longer, strong and muscular; the shoes were polished to a high shine. The high-crowned hat was held in one strong hand.

'Oh, Feargal,' his sister whispered, 'you look so—elegant. You'll break all the girl's hearts—if you haven't done so already.'

'And you look—out of this world.' He behaved as though he hadn't seen Ellie, as though she didn't exist, and she felt a lump come into her throat, felt hurt, and diminished, which was so stupid.

Extending his hand to his sister, he added, 'The car's here. Ready?'

Taking a deep breath, Terry nodded, and as though she too had forgotten Ellie she walked slowly towards her brother and out through the door.

Pulling a funny little face, telling herself it really didn't matter, that soon she would be gone, and it would all be forgotten, Ellie quickly tidied Terry's room and walked out, quietly closing the door. Would she ever get married? she wondered. See love and happiness shining in her own eyes? Perhaps. One day. But it wouldn't be Feargal. And why did it have to be this man above all others who made her heart beat that little bit faster? Out of all the men who had liked her and wanted her, why did it have to be someone who thought her the most despicable of all cheats who made her yearn for something more? Letting all her breath out on an achingly shaky sigh, and telling herself firmly to pull herself together, that seeing a bride always made her feel weepy and was nothing whatever to do with Feargal, she walked along the landing to stare from the end window. She saw them come out, saw Feargal give a wide, devilish grin, before handing Terry into the gleaming white car, saw him carefully join her—and Ellie wanted not to be here when they got back. Wanted to disappear and never have to see him again.

'Ellie? Oh, there you are!' Rose exclaimed. 'We're just off, nipping out the back way to get to the church before them. Are you coming?'

'No, I'll wait and make sure everything's ready for when they get back.'

'Are you sure?' she asked, sounding dubious.

'Yes, go on, off you go; you'll be late.'

With a nod, Rose hurried down to join her sister and Ellie heard the back door slam as they hurried out.

Walking along to her room, she quietly closed the door. Standing at the window that looked over the grounds, she thought back over her short stay here in the house, tried to see how it might have been different—and then gave a wry, sad little smile. Fool, Ellie; come on, get yourself ready, pin a smile on your face. Only another few hours to get through. Yeah. And then you too can leave. Go home. To what? Unemployment and loneliness? Better that than this—emptiness. This might-have-been. Impatient with herself, she went to shower and put on her red velvet dress. To hell with Feargal. It was a wedding. A joyous occasion, and she was damned well going to enjoy herself!

If her smile wasn't quite as enchanting as usual, her vivacity a little bit forced, it went quite unnoticed by the happy, laughing group that returned to the house. And if Feargal wanted to pretend that she didn't exist, well, who the hell cared? Taking her place for the wedding breakfast, at the table that glistened with crystal, warm with red roses, she manfully ate her way through course after course of a meal prepared by top-class chefs, listened to the speeches, the congratulations, applauded, smiled, chatted with apparent good humour. It was almost as though she stood outside herself, seeing it all through different eyes. She watched the well-dressed women with their fantastic hats, the elegant men; drank the champagne she was poured, fielded questions about herself; smiled at the teasing over her unusual dress. Unusual was perhaps the kindest word one could use. It looked like somebody's curtains cut up—which was what it probably was—and if it provided a talking-point—well, that was all to the good, wasn't it? She kept her eyes lowered when Feargal stood to speak, because if he glanced at her, and she saw contempt in his eyes, she would probably lose her temper, and that wouldn't be fair, not on Terry's day. He spoke easily, humorously, as though speech-making was a part of his everyday life. Which perhaps it was. She knew very little about him after all, had no idea what he did when he went to Dublin, or Kildare.

And when the toasts had all been made, and the cutting of the magnificent four-tiered cake was over, the photographs taken, they all spilled into the rest of the house while the tables were cleared. Feeling in dire need of fresh air, Ellie went outside into the grounds. Blue was still howling his sorrow to the world, and she slipped in to comfort him. 'Never mind, boy, it'll soon all be over and you can be comfortable again.'

Unfortunately, because he had had a source of comfort, the moment Ellie left to go back to the house his mournful howls increased in volume.

'Sure and doesn't he sound desperate?' Rose exclaimed as Ellie walked into the kitchen.

'Blue? Yes, I'm afraid that was my fault. I slipped in to see if he was all right. Do you need any help?' she offered impulsively.

'I do not! You're a guest. Go and enjoy yourself. Go on!' Shooing her out of the kitchen, Rose gave a smile when Ellie laughingly protested.

Walking into the hall, she halted as she saw Donal and a small dark-haired girl being admitted. So he'd been invited, had he? A determined look in her eye, she made a bee-line for him.

'Yes, you do well to look wary, Donal. I want a word with you!'

'Why?' he asked with a laugh that was definitely false. 'You obviously got here OK.'

'Oh, yes, I certainly got here.'

'Well, why so cross? You should be thanking me!'

'Oh, should I? Thank you for making me look a fool? Making me look as though I follow strange men about the countryside?'

'What?'

After explaining quickly about not being able to get a bed and breakfast, of being directed to the Hall, her mouth tightened when he burst out laughing.

'Oh, my. Sorry, Ellie,' he apologised, his face still creased with amusement. 'I really and truly only meant to be helpful.'

Giving him a look of disgust, she walked away. Helpful? Standing talking with Mrs McMahon a few minutes later, she saw him capture Feargal. More apologies? she wondered cynically. And would Feargal now give him the third degree? She hoped so, hoped he was being as scathing with him as he'd been with herself. Perhaps that would teach Donal not to meddle.

For the next half-hour, while everyone filtered back into the big hall, while the musicians struck up and people began to dance, she counted off the time until the bride and groom were scheduled to leave—and when she could leave herself. Her bags were all packed and ready, the car apparently mended by Feargal; all she had to do was change, and go.

Standing at the window in the small front lounge, where a buffet had been laid out for those guests arriving late, or for people who were still hungry, she saw Feargal accompany Phena, and the man who had been her constant companion at the wedding, walk down the path. The man's hand was shaken, Phena given a hug, her suitcase put in the boot of a silver car, and the car driven away with Feargal giving a last wave. Someone else eager to leave the happy occasion. Aware of no longer being alone, Ellie turned her head. Donal was standing beside her wearing a very sheepish grin.

'Hi. Well, you look as though you're still in one piece after the interrogation,' she remarked.

'How do you know that's what it was?'

'Because I'm psychic?'

With a grimace, Donal murmured gloomily. 'He wasn't exactly ecstatic at my explanation.'

'No, I don't suppose he was.'

'Well, I don't know why!' he said, affronted. 'It didn't matter, did it? You got here, are staying here where you wanted to be!'

'True. And I assume it was your sister who told you the name of the family I was looking for?'

'Yes, of course.'

'And you knew Feargal, knew his name, knew he came from Slane, and assumed it was the same family.'

'I *knew* it was the same family,' he admitted. 'I asked around, and they were the only McMahons in Slane. I didn't do it to cause trouble, Ellie,' he protested. 'I was actually, believe it or not, trying to be helpful.'

'Mm, so you said. And provide yourself with a little amusement into the bargain?'

'Well, that too, but I just thought it would be nice to have actually met a member of the family, even if you didn't know who he was. And then when you got to Slane... Only even I couldn't have known there'd be nowhere to stay but at the Hall! And I don't think I really expected Feargal to go down to Rosslare! I mean, you wouldn't, would you? He's not the sort of man you order around!'

'No.'

'And I didn't know he'd come to the hotel to find you! How could I?' Grasping her elbow, Donal moved her out of the way of the small bridesmaid who seemed to have got over-excited and was racing around with someone's little boy. 'But what I don't understand is why he's so damned angry about it!'

With a faint smile, she repeated wryly, 'No.'

'So why was he?' he asked in exasperation.

'It's a long story, and it's not really important. Not any more.'

'It isn't?' he asked with obvious disappointment.

'No.'

'You fancied him, though, didn't you?' he teased slyly.

'Did I? Perhaps.'

'Ellie!'

'What?'

'Don't be so irritating!'

'Then stop being nosy.' With a friendly pat on his arm, she went off to join the dancing, and practically walked into the waiting Feargal. 'Excuse me,' she said frostily.

'No. I want to talk to you.'

'Well, I don't want to talk to you.'

Catching her arm, he said quietly, 'I've just been talking to Donal.'

'I know.' Twisting out of his grip, she walked away. With a winning smile at a rather bemused young man, she dragged him up to dance, and every time she saw Feargal she made off in the opposite direction. And although she wasn't stupid enough to know that he wouldn't catch up with her eventually, when his role as host was over, if not before, she had high hopes that she could escape before that eventuality. She knew he watched her, and with a pronounced glitter in his blue eyes, which boded ill, but she didn't care. The days were long gone when she'd wanted him to understand, believe her. Now it was too late.

When Terry went upstairs to change, Ellie went with her, and when they came down a short while later, when Terry and Declan were ready to leave, Ellie was right there beside them. The best man was driving them to the airport for their flight to Greece, and Ellie made sure she was right in the middle of the crowd as they all surged down the front path to wish them *bon voyage.*

Giving Terry a warm hug, with a quick peck on the cheek for Declan, she edged her way to the rear of the laughing, happy crowd, well out of the way of Feargal.

'Nearly over,' she kept whispering to herself, and when everyone was back inside, the music slower, the drink flowing freely, and people began to get up and sing, she slipped out through the french doors. Moving slowly, with apparent idleness, she strolled to the end of the terrace, and into the shadows. Someone, a man, began to sing an old Irish ballad, and the mournful strains of the familiar song filled the air with sadness, tugged at the emotions, and made her more determined than ever to get away quickly. Great at singing, the Irish—great altogether at wounding the heart. She wondered if Feargal could sing. Probably. He seemed to be able to do everything else. Except judge character.

Still moving slowly, intending to make her way round to the back door, up to her room, collect her belongings, then leave the same way, she caught her breath when a stealthy hand caught hold of her arm.

CHAPTER EIGHT

'GOING SOMEWHERE, ELLIE?' Feargal asked softly.

Turning slowly towards him, she stared up into his moonlit face. 'Yes. Home,' she said quietly.

'Then before you do, will you give me five minutes of your time?'

'A request, Feargal?' she asked tartly. 'Not an order?'

'Not an order,' he agreed. Tugging her gently, he seated her on the low stone wall. 'I always trust to my instincts,' he began, his voice still soft. 'Always. And the one time I didn't was the one time I was wrong. And it was the one time that it mattered more than anything else.'

Staring out over the moon-washed garden, she refused to answer. She heard the clink of glasses being placed on the wall, heard the rustle of clothing as he removed his jacket and placed it warmly round her shoulders. A glass of champagne was held before her, and, with a little shrug, she took it. He sat beside her, close enough for her to feel the heat from his body.

'Talk to me, Ellie,' he urged quietly.

'No. No more talking.' Staring idly down into her glass, she watched the bubbles rise.

His sigh sounded long, and really rather weary. 'Then I will. At first I had no real suspicions, just a mild curiosity to see this young woman whom Donal enthused about. Although I have to confess I wondered *why* he kept telling me about you. However, seeing as I was in Rosslare that day, it amused me to keep an eye out for the car he'd described. I don't think I really expected to see it, but when I did it amused me to follow you, and when you stopped in Wexford it was idle curiosity that prompted my behaviour, nothing else.'

'Except boredom,' she couldn't resist adding.

'Mm, and boredom,' he agreed. 'So I watched you for a while, and when you saw me watching, and you looked nervous, as though you thought me a criminal, about to steal all the stock, it amused me to tease you, try and discover why Donal thought you special. And I have to admit that I found you delightful. Different. I knew you were heading for Dublin, knew which hotel, because Donal had made a great point of telling me, and so, when the dinner I was at proved to be as boring and interminable as I had known it would, I left. Dolores insisted on accompanying me, and because that was what I was supposed to be doing, escorting her, I didn't raise any objections. And I have to confess that I found you as delightful then as I had in Wexford, and was intending to find out where you were going, and pursue the acquaintanceship. Only then you turned up on my doorstep with some rigmarole about Sadie, and I was disappointed, because I didn't want you to be like all the rest. You professed your innocence . . .'

'And it amused you to see how far I would go,' she finished for him.

'Yes, and you proved to be a warm and funny companion, gentle and sweet, and I was intrigued to discover why someone like you would pursue a man. From the little I knew of you it seemed out of character. However, I'd been duped before . . .'

'So cynicism won the day.'

'Mm.'

'So, in the romantic setting of Bettystown beach, you reluctantly made it clear to your fair companion that it was goodbye and thank you. And what did the mercenary little baggage do then? Why, produce her trump card. The letters. And my, how wonderful it was to be proved right once again!'

'Yes,' he admitted.

'To achieve all her aims, stay in the house of the much sought-after man in all Ireland! And, an added bonus, in the house of the woman who'd been seduced by her grandfather! What a good joke! And, to actually get to meet her new aunty!' Draining her glass, she handed it back to him, got to her feet, and walked off. She didn't get very far.

He'd obviously put his own glass down, because he halted her by grabbing her shoulders and bringing her to a halt. Holding her stiff body in front of him, he continued quietly, 'Cynicism robs you of reason; did you know that? Robs you of sense. It seemed eminently believable that you, or possibly your family, had been annoyed, devastated—whatever—on finding out that your grandfather had been playing around with a young Irish girl, and had sent you over to demand an explanation, exact retribution...'

'Because hasn't history proved that the English are always trying to do the Irish down?'

'No, it doesn't; don't be absurd. It had nothing to do with your being English! But you didn't demand,' he continued, 'wouldn't even admit it was your grandfather who'd been responsible, which had me in a puzzle. So then I decided, reluctantly, that the letters were merely to gain introduction to the family.'

'Boy, do you have a persecution complex!'

'So would you have if you'd had to put up with half of what I've been through in the past! You accused me of being blinkered, but you're just as bad, won't even try to understand it from my point of view.'

Swinging round to face him, she demanded furiously, 'Did you try to see it from mine?'

'No,' he admitted, 'but then you don't have a sister like Phena, do you? It's like living on a time bomb! Waiting for the explosion, for it all to start up over again, terrified she would find out.'

'Terrified?' she scoffed. 'You've never been terrified in your life!'

'How do you know? I'm terrified now, terrified that you'll walk away without forgiveness . . .'

'Oh, I'm really likely to believe that, aren't I?'

'The way you're likely to believe that I had a sneaking admiration, a liking for this little harbinger of bad news? I didn't want to be beguiled by your smile, Ellie—and yet, against my will, I was. And you still,' he tacked on softly, 'despite all the evidence, don't believe it was your grandfather, do you?'

Staring at him in mild shock, she quickly lowered her lashes. Wriggling free, she walked on towards the back door, Feargal following her every step.

'Do you?' he persisted.

She ignored him, refusing to answer, because what could she say? It wasn't her secret; it belonged to his mother, one she had promised not to tell. Mounting the stairs, aware of him behind her, she walked along to her room.

'Not going to answer me, Ellie?'

'No.' Opening her door, she edged inside and tried to close it. Feargal's foot prevented her. With a shrug that she hoped looked uncaring, she walked in, removed his jacket that was still round her shoulders, picked up the jeans and shirt she had left out to change into, and went into the bathroom. Quickly changing, bundling up the red dress, she emerged to find him sitting on her bed. Ignoring him, she shoved the dress into the case, zipped it shut, and only then realised he had Gwen Bear. Holding out her hand, she waited.

'She doesn't have to leave,' he informed her, his mouth quirked engagingly.

'Yes, she does!' Snatching her bear out of his hand, Ellie tucked her under her arm. Grabbing up her handbag, she picked up her case, and staggered to the door.

'Don't you want to know what happened to Phena?' he asked softly. 'I saw you watching us from the window.'

'No,' she denied stonily.

'She's decided to marry Peter Noonan. The man she was with. He's Canadian. She's been putting him off for years. And why did she accept him now, do I hear you ask? Why, because she couldn't bear to acknowledge the legitimate granddaughter of her father...'

Dropping her suitcase with a thud, Ellie whirled round to face him. 'You bastard! Don't you dare lay that on me!'

'Why? You are her niece, aren't you?'

'No!'

'No?'

'Yes! Oh!' Grabbing up her suitcase, then finding she couldn't open the door, she thumped it down again, opened the door, then dragged it out.

'Going to make me follow you to England, Ellie?' he called softly.

'What?' Turning round, she stared at him as he lounged back on her bed.

'Well, it will be a bit difficult to court you if I'm over here and you're over there.'

'Court? Court? You wouldn't know how to court a— a courtesan!'

His lips twitching, he rolled easily to his feet and walked towards her.

Hastily slamming the door on him, because she didn't damn well want to be beguiled by his blasted charm, because it was too late, she began to hurriedly lug her suitcase down the stairs. The little group of guests gathered at the bottom looked marginally startled by her somewhat unorthodox behaviour, and she gave them a lame smile. She could hear Feargal treading softly down behind her, could imagine the stupid grin on his face, and, with a last determined effort, she humped her suitcase to the front door.

'Allow me,' Feargal said softly as he reached over her shoulder to open the door.

'Thank you,' she gritted.

'Feargal!' Mrs McMahon called in astonishment as she emerged from the lounge. 'What on earth is going on? And why is Ellie dragging her suitcase out the front door? Is she leaving?' she asked worriedly.

'No,' he denied. Scooping the suitcase out of Ellie's hand, he assisted her down the front steps towards her car.

'I am,' she contradicted.

'Of course you are,' he soothed.

Coming to a halt, she glared at him. 'Then why did you tell your mother I wasn't?'

'Because I'm an awful liar?'

'It won't work, Feargal,' she warned. 'I'm not staying.'

'Am I trying to make you?' he asked mildly.

With a pathetic little 'hmph!' she twitched away towards her car. 'And it had better start,' she muttered.

'It will.'

'Good.' Wrenching up the boot, she waited for him to put the suitcase inside, then, still hugging Gwen Bear, walked round to the driver's side and climbed in. Shoving the key in the ignition, she twisted it, and, much to her surprise—and perhaps disappointment?— it started first time.

Pushing it into first, she was just about to let off the handbrake when he opened the passenger door and awkwardly lowered his length into the small car.

'And what do you think you're doing?' she demanded frostily.

'Coming with you, of course.'

'You are not!'

'Am,' he said softly, that wretched grin pulling at his mouth.

'But why?' she wailed.

'You know why. I want to know all there is to know about an astonishingly beautiful girl called Ellie. I want to know what made her stay in the face of my behaviour, what made her help his sister when anyone else would have left her to look a fright on her wedding day...'

'No, she wouldn't,' she denied. 'You'd have found a dressmaker!'

'And what made her run his mother in to Dublin to change her wedding outfit, a woman, moreover, who'd blackened the character of her beloved grandfather.'

'What?' she whispered.

'He wasn't Phena's father, was he? No,' he confirmed gently when she just stared at him in shock, 'you needn't answer, not if you promised not to. We haven't used you very well, have we, Ellie? None of us?' Framing her tired little face with his warm palms, he dropped a kiss on her exquisite nose. 'We don't deserve another chance... I don't deserve another chance—but I'm hoping, praying that you will give me one anyway.'

'Why?'

'Because it took me such a long time to find you.'

'Find me?' she echoed stupidly.

'Mm. And if you insist on rushing off...'

'With you beside me?' she asked drily.

'Mm. I once voluntarily threw away something that promised to be special, and very, very wonderful, and don't intend to do so again. Only I would much prefer for us to stay here...'

'I'm sure you would...'

'Because if you force me to leave, what would I do about my wretched EC forms on milk yield with which I've been wrestling? On herd sizes, on quotas, the half of which I don't understand?'

'I don't know.'

'No, nor do I, and although I might have wanted, so very many times, over the past few years, to walk away, shed my responsibilities, let them all get the hell on with it, perhaps I'm a marginally better person than I had thought, because I found I couldn't do it. And now Terry has gone and there's only Mother to cope with— and a long, sterile life looming in front of me—without my little Ellie, who briefly brought some sunshine in. And,' he continued softly, his face suddenly very close to hers, 'you made a few wrong moves yourself, so this muddle is partly your fault too.'

'Oh, I might have guessed it would be,' she agreed. 'Well, go on, then; how was it my fault?'

'You took your eyes off the leprechaun.'

'Ah. So I did.'

Lines of humour fanned out from his mouth, and his teeth gleamed whitely in the darkness. 'And after me warning you, too. So, instead of heading for the ferry port, why don't we drive down to my little house in the Wicklow Mountains?'

'Why would we want to do that?' she asked softly.

'Because it would be an awful waste of a packed suitcase if we didn't at least go somewhere.'

'True.'

'You turn left at the end of the drive,' he prompted slyly.

The little curl of warmth in her stomach spread outwards and upwards, and, without giving herself time to think, she released the handbrake and followed his soft directions.

'Want me to drive?'

'No,' she denied thickly.

It took a little under an hour, and when, at his instruction, she pulled up outside a small, dark cottage she thought she felt sick.

'Not going to get out?' he asked softly.

'No, yes...' Turning towards him, she gabbled, 'Feargal, I...'

Leaning across her, he removed the keys from the ignition. 'Just in case,' he breathed against her face. Unlatching his door, groaning as he uncramped his long legs, he walked round to let her out.

'I don't...I...'

Scooping her up in his arms, he carried her towards the front door, easily unlatched it, flicked a switch, kicked the door shut behind him, and carried her into the bedroom. The light from the hall spilled across the multi-coloured counterpane, and he laid her gently in the middle. Unlacing her boots, he put them tidily on the floor, then kicked off his own shoes, removed his cravat, unhooked the top button of his shirt, and joined her on the bed.

Leaning up on one arm, not touching her, just looking into her face, he began quietly, 'Up until I was thirty, with a few exceptions, I thought I had everything I wanted, needed. Footloose and fancy-free. I pitied friends who were married, had children, were tied. But then, slowly, bit by bit, year by year, I began to change my mind. I wanted, suddenly, someone to come home to. Someone who would love me, whom I could love. Someone who would smile when I walked into a room, look pleased that I had come home—not because they wanted something from me, but because I was me. And I couldn't find her, Ellie. And then, one day, I watched a girl in Wexford market. Watched her happy smile, her gentle humour, her comical confusion, and I wanted her. Not smart, elegant, sophisticated, but eminently lovable. So I walked up to her, looked into her eyes, and close to she was as beautiful and warm as she'd seemed from a distance. And so began a chain of events, of misunderstandings, laughter, anger, and bitter recrimination. And I can't believe, looking back, that I was so monumentally stupid.' With a sigh, he touched a gentle finger to her cheek.

Staring up at him, confused and warm, but no longer frightened, yet not quite sure what to say, what response to make, she asked huskily, 'Did Phena really leave because of me?'

'In a way. You were the catalyst that she's needed all these years. She's always been afraid, I think, to fully make a life for herself, in case she was missing out, in case it all changed. Peter Noonan has been patiently waiting in the wings for six years, and finally, whether it was seeing Terry so happy, realising that she wasn't getting any younger, or the fact that I told her I was thinking of getting married, sh—'

'What?'

'Married,' he repeated. 'She finally accepted Peter's proposal.'

And because she wasn't quite ready to challenge his statement, ask him exactly what he meant, Ellie asked stupidly, 'Will she be happy?'

Amused by her prevarication, he nodded gently. 'I hope so. Pray that the bitterness will finally go. And perhaps partly it was my fault. Perhaps I handled it all wrong. But she was older than me, my big sister, so when Dad died that age difference made it difficult. Suddenly, I was the—leader, if you like, and she resented it. Resenting my making decisions that she felt she ought to make. Have you ever been in love, Ellie?' he asked, bringing them gently back on to the track he wanted.

'No,' she whispered.

'No? And does that mean . . . ?'

Knowing exactly what he was asking, she nodded. 'I didn't want there to be any half-measures, didn't want to make love to someone just for the sake of it. There needed to be a—spark, and there never was.'

'And is there a spark now?' he asked so very, very softly.

Staring up at him, she gave a jerky little nod.

'Oh, Ellie. I keep remembering how it felt to hold you in my arms—like this,' he murmured as he slid his arms round her. 'How it felt to kiss you . . .'

Closing her eyes, she melted into his embrace, willingly parted her mouth for him—and she truly hadn't known, until now, how many ways there were to kiss—or what a gloriously long time it would take to discover them all. His arms stayed warmly round her, held her loosely. His hands didn't roam, didn't take liberties that she might not have wanted him to take; only his head moved, his mouth, as he kissed her first one way, then another; drew her lower lip, infinitely gently, between his; sampled the top lip, her tongue; moved languidly to approach from another direction. It was slow, dreamlike, and unbelievably beautiful—erotic and exciting.

Feeling drugged, and wanton, she touched her fingers to his nape, his ears, tangled them in his thick hair, felt his soft sigh as his breath mingled with hers—and still he continued to kiss her. There were brief explorations across her warm, soft cheek, her eyes, her nose, but always, always, he returned to that sweet source that he seemed to find so fascinating—until eventually, light-years later, he lifted his head.

Raising lids that felt too heavy, she stared up into his face. 'I didn't know,' she began dazedly, 'that just kissing could produce such . . . make me feel so . . .'

'No,' he agreed as he smoothed one large palm across her short hair, moved to cup her face. 'You're so exquisitely warm, and soft, so unbelievably beautiful—and I want your love, your babies—your life.'

Unable to move, unable to speak, she stared at his perfectly shaped mouth, unconsciously licked her dry lips.

'*Grá mo chroí,*' he whispered thickly.

'What does that mean?' she managed shakily.

'Love of my heart.'

With a fluttery little breath, she whispered, 'Oh, Feargal. You sound so sure.'

'I am sure. But you aren't, are you? How could you be when I've shown you nothing but contempt?' His fingers warm against her cheek, as though he needed to touch, he continued, 'When you've wanted something for so long, and you finally think you've found it, and then it all turns to ashes, it makes you over-react— sounds lame, doesn't it? But you have the power to hurt me, Ellie, and because I knew that I masochistically invited more. Nothing new about that, is there?' He smiled. 'Lovers all through history have consistently screwed up their lives.'

'Lovers?' she asked, savouring the word.

'Mm, please God. Lovers. One day very soon.'

'Yes,' she agreed softly as she drew his head back to hers. 'One day very soon.'

Welcome to Europe

IRELAND—'the Emerald Isle'

Go to Eire and you open the door on a hauntingly beautiful land in which the 18th century elegance of the capital city complements the whitewashed stone cottages studding the sweeping countryside around it, and where donkey carts travel the roads in between. You and your lover will feel its own special warmth and welcome envelop you wherever you go as you soak up the magic of Eire.

THE ROMANTIC PAST...

The hills and valleys of Eire are littered with ancient monuments of the Stone, Bronze and Iron Ages, relics that have been surrounded by romantic myth and legend by the Celtic storytellers and which are now carefully preserved as the country's precious heritage. An example is the **Brugh Na Bóinne** area, a cemetery of Stone Age kings over 2 miles long and enclosed by the River Boynne as a prehistoric city of the dead.

Between AD 600 and AD 900 Eire was the most civilised part of Europe, and evidence of this can be found in Dublin's **National Museum,** displaying the skills of ancient craftsmen—the exquisite Tara brooch is among the treasures. The famous **Book of Kells,** an illustrated manuscript dating from AD 800, is to be seen in the Trinity College Library.

The name **Dublin** comes from the Irish Dubhlinn ('dark pool'), and she recently celebrated her 1,000th birthday, having been captured from the Vikings in AD 988.

Dublin has produced many great writers—**Sheridan, Wilde** and **Goldsmith,** as well as **G. B. Shaw,** whose statue stands outside the National Gallery. A host of others, such as **Yeats, James Joyce** and **Samuel Beckett,** drew much inspiration from the city, a centre of the cultural movement in the late 18th century.

Jonathan Swift, most famous for his *Gulliver's Travels,* was dean of St Patrick's Cathedral, Dublin, for over 30 years. In 1742 he presided at the first public performance of Handel's *Messiah* while the composer was visiting the city. Swift's romances live on in his writing: *Journal to Stella* reveals his longing to be with her in the peace and tranquillity of rural Meath, and the poem 'Cadenus and Vanessa' is the result of a stormy affair with Esther Vanhomrigh, who followed him to Dublin after falling madly in love with him in London.

Tara in Meath was once the centre of Irish power and a source of many vivid tales. The festivals held here thrice yearly in Roman times included ritual marriages between the king and maidens. In its banqueting hall begins one of the most famous local stories, that of Diarmuid and Gráinne, a tale of love and betrayal, high chivalry, the loyalty of comrades and the fickleness and wiles of one woman. It inspired W. B. Yeats to write his 'Lullaby'.

Legend has it that frogs, toads and snakes were expelled from Eire in the 5th century by St Patrick's tolling of the bell from the top of the Croagh Patrick Mountain.

If you see a **leprechaun,** it will be on a moonlit night and he'll be making shoes for fairies and sipping mountain dew. He should be approached soundlessly, taken by the hand and asked firmly where the crocks of gold are to be found; be prepared for great cunning in order for him to escape, but if this fails he will tell you!

THE ROMANTIC PRESENT—pastimes for lovers...

The cosmopolitan flavour of Dublin offers days of pleasure to the visitor—you will be overwhelmed by the grandeur of the Georgian squares at its heart, rubbing shoulders familiarly with cosy pubs and colourful markets.

To enjoy the timeless atmosphere of the capital, a stroll along **Burgh Quay** at dusk will bring you to the impressive sight of **Custom House,** its distinctive copper dome illuminated against the skyline; during the day one of the best places to relax is **Trinity College Park,** where you can admire the imposing façade of the college itself, as well as that of **Parliament House,** now the Bank of Ireland and holding many interesting exhibitions.

Bustling Dublin is never far away, and in **Moore Street** you will find a thriving fruit and vegetable market, while for clothes, jewellery, books and bric-a-brac the **Dandelion Market** through the Gaiety Green Arcade is very good. The city has a growing reputation as an excellent shopping centre, based on the wealth of fine fashion shops, delicatessens, department stores and antique shops to be found there; you can treat yourself to gifts ranging from traditional Irish clothing and world-famous **Waterford glass** to the latest in designer clothing!

The theatrical tradition is strong in Dublin, and the famous **Abbey Theatre** specialises in Irish plays and live music—jazz, folk and rock. If you'd prefer to spend the evening in one of the city's numerous atmospheric pubs, you will probably be treated to some lively Irish entertainment while enjoying your drink! One of the most traditional is **The Bailey** in Duke Street—a pub has stood here since the 17th century and it was immortalised in Joyce's *Ulysses*.

Dublin has plenty of excellent restaurants, but wherever you go in Eire you are presented with the opportunity to sample its delicious cooking based on meat, seafood, eggs and butter. The best traditional dishes to look out for are **Irish stew**—mutton neck, onions and potatoes—**bacon and cabbage casserole, potato cakes,** home-made brown **soda bread** and **barm brack** (rich fruity bread). All, of course, washed down with a glass of **Guinness!**

No trip to Eire is complete without discovering some of its spectacular scenery: you can walk almost anywhere in the mountains behind **Carlingford** and **Omeath,** where some of the most beautiful hill-walking imaginable, in country stained with episodes of Irish legend, is at your feet. To the south is the 'garden of Ireland', **County Wicklow**, whose hills are full of streams and in whose mountain hollows are to be found deep lakes. There are over 400 forest parks to choose from in the country, and three national parks, not to mention the miles of rugged coastline and the idyllic sandy coves.

To enjoy the countryside at a relaxing pace and in unbeatable romantic style, why not hire a **horse-drawn caravan** for a few days? Though it's surely the slowest way to travel, what better way to complete your love-affair with Eire?

DID YOU KNOW THAT...?

* the **monetary unit** of Eire is the Irish pound, or *punt,* which is composed of 100 pence. The currency symbol is the pound sign (£). Irish coins are minted at the Royal Mint in London, and are of the same size and denomination as British currency.

* **Irish lace** can be bought, either in smart shops or the convents in which it is made, and long-lasting **hand-knitted sweaters** and **Donegal Tweed** are practical and attractive souvenirs. **Claddagh rings** are the best love tokens you will find, here or anywhere!

* in the Irish Republic all the **pillar-boxes** are green, and in Dublin the **street names** are in Gaelic.

* in Gaelic the words of love are *A grá mo chroí—* *'love of my heart'.*

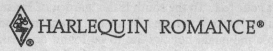

HARLEQUIN ROMANCE®

brings you

More Romances Celebrating Love, Families and Children!

Next month, look out for Emma Goldrick's new book,
Leonie's Luck, Harlequin Romance #3351
(a heart-warming story of romantic involvement between
Leonie Marshal and Charlie Wheeler, who marches
without warning—or permission—into her life!)

Charlie's nine-year-old daughter, Cecilia, who comes to
live with them—at Leonie's Aunt Agnes's invitation—is
somehow never far from what is going on and plays an
innocent part in bringing them together!

Available wherever Harlequin books are sold.

Take 4 bestselling love stories FREE

Plus get a FREE surprise gift!

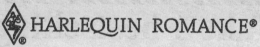

HARLEQUIN ROMANCE®

Last month we announced our Sealed with a Kiss series, which starts in March. This is just to tell you about our choice for that month which we know you will love!

Invitation to Love is the story of Heidi who needs to make a living for herself, but when that livelihood involves welcoming into her home handsome Dillon Archer—the man she believes caused her father's death—she's forced to swallow her pride!

Don't miss Harlequin Romance #3352
Invitation to Love
by Leigh Michaels

Available in March, wherever Harlequin books are sold.

SWAK-1

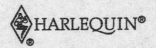

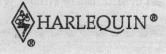

Fifty red-blooded, white-hot, true-blue hunks
from every State in the Union!

Look for MEN MADE IN AMERICA! Written by some
of our most popular authors, these stories feature some
of the strongest, sexiest men, each from a different state
in the union!

Two titles available every month at your favorite
retail outlet.

In February, look for:

THE SECURITY MAN by Dixie Browning
(North Carolina)
A CLASS ACT by Kathleen Eagle (North Dakota)

In March, look for:

TOO NEAR THE FIRE by Lindsay McKenna (Ohio)
A TIME AND A SEASON by Curtiss Ann Matlock
(Oklahoma)

You won't be able to resist MEN MADE IN AMERICA!

HARLEQUIN®

Don't miss these Harlequin favorites by some of our most distinguished authors!
And now, you can receive a discount by ordering two or more titles!

HT#25577	WILD LIKE THE WIND by Janice Kaiser	$2.99	☐
HT#25589	THE RETURN OF CAINE O'HALLORAN by JoAnn Ross	$2.99	☐
HP#11626	THE SEDUCTION STAKES by Lindsay Armstrong	$2.99	☐
HP#11647	GIVE A MAN A BAD NAME by Roberta Leigh	$2.99	☐
HR#03293	THE MAN WHO CAME FOR CHRISTMAS by Bethany Campbell	$2.89	☐
HR#03308	RELATIVE VALUES by Jessica Steele	$2.89	☐
SR#70589	CANDY KISSES by Muriel Jensen	$3.50	☐
SR#70598	WEDDING INVITATION by Marisa Carroll	$3.50 U.S. $3.99 CAN.	☐
HI#22230	CACHE POOR by Margaret St. George	$2.99	☐
HAR#16515	NO ROOM AT THE INN by Linda Randall Wisdom	$3.50	☐
HAR#16520	THE ADVENTURESS by M.J. Rodgers	$3.50	☐
HS#28795	PIECES OF SKY by Marianne Willman	$3.99	☐
HS#28824	A WARRIOR'S WAY by Margaret Moore	$3.99 U.S. $4.50 CAN.	☐

(limited quantities available on certain titles)

	AMOUNT	$
DEDUCT:	**10% DISCOUNT FOR 2+ BOOKS**	$
ADD:	**POSTAGE & HANDLING**	$
	($1.00 for one book, 50¢ for each additional)	
	APPLICABLE TAXES*	$_____
	TOTAL PAYABLE	$_____
	(check or money order—please do not send cash)	

To order, complete this form and send it, along with a check or money order for the total above, payable to Harlequin Books, to: **In the U.S.:** 3010 Walden Avenue, P.O. Box 9047, Buffalo, NY 14269-9047; **In Canada:** P.O. Box 613, Fort Erie, Ontario, L2A 5X3.

Name: _____

Address: _____ City: _____

State/Prov.: _____ Zip/Postal Code: _____

*New York residents remit applicable sales taxes.
 Canadian residents remit applicable GST and provincial taxes.

HBACK-JM2